D1037926

MY MRS. BROWN

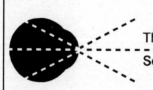

This Large Print Book carries the
Seal of Approval of N.A.V.H.

My Mrs. Brown

William Norwich

THORNDIKE PRESS
A part of Gale, Cengage Learning

GALE
CENGAGE Learning·

Farmington Hills, Mich • San Francisco • New York • Waterville, Maine
Meriden, Conn • Mason, Ohio • Chicago

GALE
CENGAGE Learning®

Copyright © 2015 by Great Blue Heron, Inc.
Thorndike Press, a part of Gale, Cengage Learning.

ALL RIGHTS RESERVED
This book is a work of fiction. Any references to historical events, real people, or real places are used fictitiously. Other names, characters, places, and events are products of the author's imagination, and any resemblance to actual events or places or persons, living or dead, is entirely coincidental.

Thorndike Press® Large Print Women's Fiction
The text of this Large Print edition is unabridged.
Other aspects of the book may vary from the original edition.
Set in 16 pt. Plantin.

LIBRARY OF CONGRESS CATALOGING-IN-PUBLICATION DATA

Names: Norwich, William, author.
Title: My Mrs. brown / by William Norwich.
Description: Large print edition. | Waterville, Maine : Thorndike Press, 2016. | © 2016 | Series: Thorndike Press large print women's fiction
Identifiers: LCCN 2016012350 | ISBN 9781410490599 (hardcover) | ISBN 1410490599 (hardcover)
Subjects: LCSH: Large type books.
Classification: LCC PS3564.O778 M9 2016b | DDC 813/.54—dc23
LC record available at http://lccn.loc.gov/2016012350

Published in 2016 by arrangement with Simon & Schuster, Inc.

Printed in Mexico
1 2 3 4 5 6 7 20 19 18 17 16

*For mothers and mentors, and
especially for L.G. in memoriam*

In the midst of winter, I found there was, within me, an invincible summer.

— ALBERT CAMUS

CHAPTER 1

Early one September not long ago, a rural woman with a secret grief traveled to New York City in pursuit of a dream, to buy the most beautiful and correct dress she'd ever seen.

The occasion wasn't a joy trip. Without tremendous effort before her trip, and a lot of luck, the dress was hardly anything she could have ever afforded. As for going to New York City, where she'd never been before? It was a terrifying prospect, dangerous and disorienting, but she did it.

The dress wasn't at all what you might expect. It wasn't a riot of feathers and chiffon. It wasn't designed to catch a man or reawaken her youth. It had nothing to do with a paparazzi-lined red carpet or the glories of shopping, "It" bags, "It" designers, or must-haves. The dress — and the lady's use for it — was something else.

This daring voyager was Emilia Brown, or

Mrs. Brown as she was generally known in her hometown, Ashville, Rhode Island. She was sixty-six years old, a widow; if she was a scent, she was tea with honey, but if she was a color, she was a study in gray. Whether from the friction of living without life's buffering luxuries and engaging ambitions, or by the reduction of dreams and expectations that comes with age: gray. Mrs. Brown was drained of color. Except for her green-brown eyes. If and when she smiled, well, it was like watching a rose open in one of those time-lapse films, and her eyes, spring flowers at twilight, lit up her face.

To say that she was overall gray isn't to say she was a sad sight or threadbare. It's just that in a world where status is measured in how much space one takes up and how much noise one makes — and noise takes up its own kind of space, as any pollution does — a quiet person like Mrs. Brown falls invisible.

Mrs. Brown was genteel. That's not a word used much anymore, except maybe when people talk about some of the characters on PBS shows. As it relates to Mrs. Brown, it signifies a graceful way, someone free from vulgarity and rudeness. Aristocratic in a manner having nothing to do with money, fame, and celebrity.

Nor is saying that someone is genteel necessarily the same as saying that someone is humble. We put so much stock and pride in being humble these days that humility has become a brand, not a state of grace.

Mrs. Brown has a noble spirit — the honorable loneliness of the American grown-up. A life sustained by quietude and the energies of tolerance, kindness, courtesy, and acceptance. In a blustery world, it's courageous to move quietly, claiming few, if any, treasures except one's solitary dignity.

She was not a career woman, hadn't been to college; she had always worked. Hers were always blue-collar jobs — a Thermos factory before it went bust, cleaning houses, babysitting, taking in washing and sewing. She was a very good seamstress, as was her mother, who had taught her how to sew and to make clothes using inexpensive Simplicity and Vogue patterns. Most recently her job was the cleaning up and helping out, six days a week, seven to seven, at Bonnie's Beauty Salon on the main street in Ashville.

A good three hours from Boston, and at least five hours from New York, Ashville wasn't a suburb of any city. Its residents relied on the local economy for their living, the stores, the businesses, and Guilford College, one of the oldest in the country. No

11

one had gotten rich in Ashville in decades, but most felt that they were well compensated nonetheless by the lasting Currier & Ives patina of their village, founded in 1649.

Here Mrs. Brown was born, an only child. In Ashville she had met and married her late husband. Older by some ten years than she, Jack Brown was a fireman for the Ashville Fire Department. He died fifteen years ago. Heart attack in his sleep.

Everyone said it was the best way to go, never sick for a day then, pop — you up and leave this mortal coil. Everyone said Jack Brown had gone easier into his death than anything he'd ever done in his uphill life.

Mrs. Brown made do. Financially, emotionally, she made do. As one does.

She avoided excesses of any sort — shopping, overeating, drinking, feelings, and lottery tickets.

Especially lottery tickets. It wasn't because she was risk averse, but because lottery tickets were bedazzlements possessed by expectation. Buying them overexcited the ladies at the beauty salon. Customers and employees alike, chattering a mile a minute, screaming to be heard over hair blowers, describing how and where they would spend the money. Then the next day, crashing so low when they didn't win.

Mrs. Brown tried never to let a tear to drop. (Of course tears dropped, in private, late at night, in the morning light when shadows haunt.) If she never expected too much, she'd never be bankrupted by disappointment.

This was all very New England of her.

Mrs. Brown didn't have a "bucket list," and she never shopped to cheer herself up. She had her clothes for years and had made the majority of them — a few pairs of pants — gray, black, brown summer and winter weight — a couple of wool or cotton cardigan sweaters, cotton blouses — and wore them for the duration, repairing them when needed. Sewing cheered her up, and helped restore her universe to order, one concentrated stitch at a time.

And although she was good-looking enough — her Yankee slender, high cheekbones and her healthy skin, her hair always clean and brushed — she did not encourage anyone, including the gentlemen, to look.

She took care of herself, but never indulged. Even when Mrs. Brown was most tempted, when it would be so lovely not to cook — so wonderful in the dead of winter to walk home after work carrying a warm supper in her hands — she never bought the costly takeaway food from the Village Cheese Shop. No restaurant dining either. She always ate at home, always cooked at home.

Dull?

Mrs. Brown never took vacations. The big cities she had visited were Providence, one hour away, and Hartford, two hours away. As mentioned, she had never been to New York City, although, admittedly, sometimes those advertisements on the television for Broadway musicals were tempting.

Who Mrs. Brown was, her vocation if you will, was to be a good person and to live an ordered, simple life.

When a student at Guilford College came by Bonnie's one day doing a survey about women's rights, she asked Mrs. Brown if she considered herself a feminist.

Mrs. Brown smiled and answered that, yes, she did.

The college girl seemed surprised.

"Liberated not always by circumstances that I'd have chosen for myself," Mrs. Brown said.

"What's your first name?" the student asked so she could put it on her survey sheet.

"Mrs.," answered Mrs. Brown.

"Your first name is . . ."

"Mrs."

The college student didn't know how to respond. "Mrs.?" She wouldn't forget Mrs. Brown anytime soon.

Keeping grateful was essential to Mrs. Brown. But she didn't need to write a "gratitude list." Gratitude was an energy she could summon up on a daily basis, grateful for what she had and for what remained after so many years of the rumble and the tumble.

One major contributor to her gratitude was that she owned her own house, a cozy two-unit wood-shingled nest built at the turn of the twentieth century, when Ashville's mills and factories were thriving. Sure it was just like all the other houses on her street — except this one was hers. She thought it lovely, all she needed or wanted. And because Ashville was built on the steep, mossy banks of the Fogg River, when the leaves fell in autumn, Mrs. Brown could see the slate and brindle–colored river from her second-floor windows.

The two-story house was divided into two units. Both units had identically proportioned front rooms, kitchens, a bath, and a bedroom downstairs, and upstairs two more small bedrooms. The units shared a front stoop.

Many years ago Mrs. Brown had rented the second unit to Sarah Fox, a widow whose circumstances were similar to Mrs. Brown's. Except Mrs. Fox's purview, you might say, was wider.

Sarah Fox had been a proud salesperson at the Ashville Bookshop, until it went out of business several years ago. This is where the students from Guilford bought their textbooks until shopping online proved easier for them, and this is where Mrs. Fox, who started working at the bookshop when she was a high school junior, tried to be more than just the local source for the latest potboilers and bodice rippers but also a beacon for the advancement of literature, even the most controversial, dating back to that frigid Saturday morning in 1969 when she insisted bravely to the waspish owner of the store that Mr. Philip Roth's novel *Portnoy's Complaint* should not only be available upon request at the cash register but also displayed proudly in the front window of the store.

Mrs. Fox felt it was always important to be up to speed on not just the latest books but also movies, television, and current events. She'd been to New York several

16

times. She longed to go to Paris before she died.

Most recently, she had gone all the way to Vancouver, Canada, when Clara, the eldest of her two children, daughters in their forties now — had asked her to please come help care for Clara's first grandchild, and Mrs. Fox's first great-grandchild, a boy named Aaron. Sadly, but sadly not uncommon, Aaron's mother and father, emotionally unprepared for parenthood, had split soon after he was born. The young mother was heartbroken, back at her work by day, bookkeeping and scheduling service appointments for a Land Rover car dealership, and thoroughly exhausted at night, so it became Clara's responsibility — "my opportunity," she said when she explained all this to Mrs. Fox — "to help raise my first grandchild."

But Clara needed her mother's support. Could Mrs. Fox please come to Vancouver for a few weeks to help, because Clara also worked full-time as the office manager at a cardiologist's clinic, a great job she was in no financial position to give up. Of course Mrs. Fox could, and she did, but never suspecting that a few weeks would turn into nearly a year.

In Mrs. Fox's place, Clara's youngest

17

daughter, Alice Danvers, twenty-three, had moved into her grandmother's home in Ashville. She'd come to help Mrs. Fox pack, and while so doing discovered that there was a teaching position for the second grade at the local grammar school. Alice had majored in education at college back home. Since she hadn't found a position yet in Vancouver, and she was itching to try living someplace else, Alice applied for the job in Ashville and to her amazement was hired.

"We love your grandmother," the principal said when she told Alice the good news. "I miss being able to visit her at the bookstore."

Would Alice be able to last an entire school year in Ashville? She had some very real doubts. But a job is a job, especially a first job in one's profession of choice, and the only way to get to your dream job is to start somewhere. Alice accepted the offer to teach in Ashville but with many conflicted feelings.

Ashville was, just, so . . . "effing," one of Alice's favorite words, quaint and mumsy. It was the complete opposite of where she saw herself living and working.

Could she, would she, ever fit in?

When her first day of teaching school came, she panicked. Among her chief concerns what the effing hell was she going to wear? She didn't own any floral prints and corduroy, which she assumed all the teachers would be wearing. Beware of any enterprise that requires new clothes, she'd once read. So she wore what she'd have worn wherever she was. Alice's teaching uniform consisted of a pair of black jeans, black cotton T-shirts — her favorite said I'LL STOP WEARING BLACK WHEN THEY INVENT A DARKER COLOR in big block letters across the chest — and motorcycle boots. No one at school seemed to mind.

Where Mrs. Brown and Mrs. Fox were the same age, born just two months apart and both Ashville natives, Alice and Mrs. Brown were worlds and generations apart. Nevertheless, her grandmother had asked for just one favor when she told Alice she could live in her place rent-free.

To please look in on Mrs. Brown daily, and make sure she never felt lonely or neglected.

It was the night before Mrs. Fox left for Vancouver. Alice was helping her pack.

"Emilia isn't like the women of your generation," Mrs. Fox said. She handed Alice a silk scarf with a rose print on it that she hadn't worn in years, and wasn't planning to bring to Vancouver.

19

"You tend to overshare, dear."

"What? I don't overshare, Granny," Alice said, tying the scarf around her neck. It looked very 1950s, and she liked that. It was corny and glamorous. In her all-black wardrobe it would strike a cool note of irony, she thought, especially in quaint Ashville, if anyone here would ever notice and get the message.

"Emilia is very private," Mrs. Fox said.

What was her grandmother really talking about? Alice wondered. She kept quiet, and listened.

Mrs. Fox explained further. "It's not that she is secretive, it's just that still waters run deep in Emilia."

Now whenever she spoke to her grandmother on the phone, which was usually once on the weekend and once midweek, Alice was expected to update Mrs. Fox on how Mrs. Brown was getting along. Meanwhile, Mrs. Fox and Mrs. Brown were communicating by letter, if you can believe people still do that, handwritten letters sometimes as long as three pages each.

And, so, a routine emerged for Alice that year in Ashville. As had been her grandmother's habit most evenings when Mrs. Brown got home from work, Alice sat at the older woman's table and visited, sometimes

20

eating supper, sometimes not, depending on their appetites, and always sharing the day's news.

This happened not every single night — a woman has a life, even in as small a town as Ashville — but many nights, five out of seven on average — Alice visited with Mrs. Brown. At first she did it because she'd promised her grandmother, but soon enough something about Mrs. Brown's manner — even if it was sometimes perplexing — also very much appealed to her.

The nightly visits, the ongoing narrative, and the reliable exchange of kindness between them became an anchor for Alice. They were different generations for sure, but she came to respect their differences. On many occasions Alice held her tongue — and swallowed the swearing words that otherwise peppered her vocabulary when she was speaking to her peers online or in person.

This particular evening in November, more than three months since her move to Ashville, Alice sat at Mrs. Brown's kitchen table drinking a cup of mint tea, listening to her enthuse about her day off tomorrow, actually two days off because she had worked seven straight in a row last week. Mrs. Brown was very much looking forward to assisting in the inventory taking at Millicent Groton's house. In fact, she was thrilled.

For generations Mrs. Groton's family had lived in an exquisite Federal-style house in the best part of Ashville. According to an *Architectural Digest* magazine article that Mrs. Brown had once read at the Ashville Public Library, the house had twenty-two rooms filled with important American furniture and paintings. And for as long as Mrs. Brown could remember — back when she was a little girl walking with her mother from their part of town to the finer section of Ashville for church on Sundays — the house had never failed to glisten behind its massive wrought-iron fence. The mansion was painted white as a heavenly cloud and exuded a halo of gold. It was the most majestic thing she'd ever hope to see.

Mrs. Groton's arrival every July in time for the Ashville Rose Festival — landing in a purl of grandeur like Queen Elizabeth coming home to one of her countryside properties in England — was the high point of the year for Mrs. Brown.

Mrs. Brown could not afford to buy an expensive benefit ticket for the opening ceremonies at the rose show — she was content to go two days later, when Ashville was admitted for free. But the afternoon of the opening ceremony, there always was a crowd waiting to see Mrs. Groton and her houseguests. Over the years they had rather famously included the Duchess of Windsor, Gregory Peck, Ginger Rogers, Betty Ford, Nancy Reagan, and Lady Bird Johnson. There were artists and literary people whom she didn't always recognize, but it didn't matter. Mrs. Brown trusted that they were all distinguished people. Everyone looked so grand. Shiny people. Sparkling like freshly minted silver dollars.

Since she was a schoolgirl, Mrs. Brown had made sure she got to the Rose Festival way ahead of the crowd for a good position up front, so she could watch. Let anyone try to stand in front of her, and she was atypically assertive.

For the past few summers, fearing each might be the elderly Mrs. Groton's last time at the festival, Mrs. Brown had asked Mrs. Fox to please come with her. It embarrassed Mrs. Fox, she was no one's groupie, but she went along anyway because it seemed so important to her friend.

"She's like a rose herself," Mrs. Brown had whispered to Mrs. Fox as the frail older woman, Mrs. Groton, assisted by a niece, arrived at the flower show (held on one of the village's center greens not far from the Groton homestead). As always, even in her nineties, Mrs. Groton was impeccably dressed, wearing a hat and white gloves and three-and-a-half-inch heels.

Mrs. Brown remembered that last sighting. "The thing of it is, Alice, is how comfortable in her skin Mrs. Groton was."

Alice shrugged, and sipped her tea. "That was probably very expensive skin, Mrs. Brown. You would be comfortable, too. And how many face-lifts do you think she had?"

Mrs. Brown took the question personally and was offended on behalf of the deceased. "She never had a face-lift. She just had good skin, that's all," she said, stiffly stirring her coffee. Within seconds, though, she forgave Alice. She was coming to love Alice despite the darker, sarcastic view of life she seemed to have, or at least that was the quality expressed in her humor.

With age, she expected Alice would soften. Isn't that what happens? Some people grow older and more cynical. Some people become just the opposite. Life hurts without hope, and cynicism, once a luxury, becomes unaffordable.

"The glass must always be half full, not half empty, Alice," Mrs. Brown said. "When you've bumped along as long as I have, you realize that if you're going to be happy and get any peace and satisfaction from the world, you just have to begin seeing that the glass is half full and refilling itself all the time."

Alice debated getting into anything akin to an argument tonight. But she wasn't a proponent of positive thinking.

"And you know all those positive-thinking books — about things like thriving and mindfulness — you know, Mrs. Brown, that they're written by people who are rich. Easy enough for them to see everything that way, lean in and thrive, and telling everyone to repeat positive-thinking memes . . ."

"Memes?" Mrs. Brown asked.

"Ideas that you spread," Alice said.

"But, Alice, you don't affirm thoughts and positive thinking to convince yourself of something. You do it to remind yourself these sayings are true."

Why argue? Alice changed the subject, slightly.

"I just think for tomorrow you should try not to have high expectations of anything. You don't know who will be there, and for all you do know, if there are a lot of city people — auction house experts and the like — they might not let you even see the house and put you somewhere, like in a garage, where you are just packing up bits in boxes."

"I know that, Alice. Really, I do," said Mrs. Brown.

She remembered when she was seven years old. That year at the Rose Festival was the first time she ever saw Mrs. Groton. She didn't know who it was; she thought Mrs. Groton was Glinda, the good witch in *The Wizard of Oz.*

She was in awe, total awe.

She'd seen the film only months before, in its first telecast, in 1956. The beneficence, the light-colored hair, the dress that appeared to sparkle all seemed the same person.

Mrs. Brown's mother, who'd brought her child to the Rose Festival, did nothing to dissuade her daughter. Far better to have your daughter grow up admiring a woman of substance, even one with unattainable wealth, than a flighty starlet somewhere, she figured.

"How can I explain this?" Mrs. Brown paused to think. "Try this: going tomorrow to Mrs. Groton's house after all these years; I feel like Dorothy in *The Wizard of Oz* before she met the wizard. Remember?"

Alice shook her head. "He was a fake, Mrs. Brown. That's what I remember."

"No, he wasn't, Alice!" Mrs. Brown shot

back. "He was an idea. A very, very good idea!"

Later, before turning off her bedside light for sleep, Mrs. Brown thought more about Mrs. Groton.

In the 1950s, especially in small New England towns like Ashville, the most valued lives were those emblematic of honesty, purity, unselfishness, and love.

By that standard, Mrs. Groton was a woman of great value and success. People, even those who struggled for their income, forgave her wealth because it was the means by which she lived a rich life of service to her community. Happily, the people of Ashville weren't wrong in their estimation.

As so many around the country, they got to know Mrs. Groton from her published writing. Throughout the 1970s and well into the 1980s, Mrs. Groton wrote a column for one of the popular women's magazines, dispensing style and manners advice for "women of a certain age," and sharing her experiences of the world. Mrs. Brown looked forward to the twentieth of every month, give or take a few days, when she would receive in her mail the latest issue of the magazine.

Over the years Mrs. Brown had clipped and saved many of Mrs. Groton's columns.

One of her favorites was how, year after year in the magazine's Christmas issue, after Mrs. Groton suggested various ideas for presents, glittering things she'd seen in the shops, she always concluded with this spirited advice:

If you can't afford to shop this year, by all means celebrate nonetheless. Write letters to everyone on your list and tell them how and why you appreciate them, especially this year. Be specific. Cite examples. And this advice isn't just for women whose budgets preclude shopping. It's also for women who shop at the holiday, and maybe shop too much. Especially to children and grandchildren, let your note, even more than your present, be the real gift. Why not? If it is written from your heart, it's a keeper, and far more lasting than the pair of new gloves soon lost in a taxi.

Even though the people, places, and things described were not of Mrs. Brown's experience, she identified with the feelings in Mrs. Groton's columns.

There was the one about meeting Eleanor Roosevelt — "focused and determined with the kindest heart and concern for people of all races and economies."

Another column was from London, where Mrs. Groton had just met the Queen. "Talking to her, you realize that Her Majesty is at heart a young mother and wife like you once were, or may still be. But she is the most grown-up woman I've ever known. Already through so many trials and tribulations she is par excellence the most elegant survivor I expect I'll ever be so privileged to meet."

And the column Mrs. Groton wrote about her housekeeper in New York, the mother of a soldier who was killed in Vietnam.

"When a child dies, not just all mothers, but all women, become one in grief," Mrs. Groton wrote.

Everyone in Ashville understood. Mrs. Groton's only child, her son, David, had been killed in the Vietnam War the year before. Of that, she never wrote, but the depth of her feelings, and her courage, was never doubted.

David's memorial service was held at St. James' Church in New York, but he was buried in Ashville. There were a few people left, now of a certain age, including Mrs. Brown, who never forgot the hearse down Main Street the autumn day he was put to rest, the crackling sounds of the car's slow wheels on dry October leaves, and seeing

Mrs. Groton through the window, having chosen to ride with David rather than in a separate car. Her gloved hand on the flag on his coffin; keeping it in place, holding on.

CHAPTER 2

Excitement wrecked Mrs. Brown's usually sound sleep. Her mind raced, imagining what splendor she might see at Mrs. Groton's house in the morning, and worrying about what mistakes she might make. What if she broke something delicate during the inventory taking?

I'm as nervous as if I was going to Buckingham Palace, she thought, pulling the bedcovers to her nose. I'm as nervous as if I was going to the White House — not that I'd ever have to worry about that.

At 5:00 A.M. she gave up the pretense of sleeping, got up, and sat in a wood chair next to her bed. It was still dark outside. Very soon, her neighborhood would come to life, bubbling with voices, some happy, some angry, in English or Spanish mostly now, although, years ago, there was Portuguese, Greek, and when she was a little girl Yiddish.

But right now there was silence, and in the silence there were memories.

Mrs. Brown opened the drawer of her bedside table and put away the framed family photographs she displayed every night before she went to sleep.

Not that anyone ever was in her bedroom except herself, but she kept these photographs in the drawer during the day, resting in the middle of a stack of white cotton handkerchiefs, to protect them from, well, she wasn't entirely sure. Dust? She cleaned too often and there wasn't any. Sunlight? There wasn't much of that in this room either. What was she protecting? She was protecting her treasured photographs from time's most corrosive element: forgetting.

Constants in a room, lamps and tables, for example, and photographs, you can become so used to that most of the time you don't even notice they are there. But her ritual of in and out from the drawer, morning and night, helped Mrs. Brown keep her greatest treasures alive, one treasure in particular.

CHAPTER 3

She had her tea. She fed the cat, her marbled black and white companion named Santo.

Having carefully examined her outfit the night before, sewing a stitch or two where she feared a hem could possibly come undone, Mrs. Brown dressed in loose-fitting gray trousers and a brown twinset, sweater and shell, as her generation called these sleeveless wool blouses. Her mother always said that when your clothes are not rich clothes you should buy them or, in Mrs. Brown's case, make them in a larger size. The lack in the quality of the fabric doesn't show as much when the clothing is loose.

She brushed her thick gray hair from the nape of her neck and then backward again from the forehead. Mrs. Brown thought this made her look taller and more distinguished.

She did not wear makeup and used lipstick

rarely, and certainly not today, when she did not wish to look anything akin to a tart, not that she ever had or ever could.

She considered that she might try a bit of the floral-scented toilet water Mrs. Fox had given her for Christmas three, actually four years ago. She decided against it. But she would be so embarrassed if her clothes smelt of any cooking she'd done, or any household cleaning products she used, the smells she feared lingered in her house and her clothing. Her solution was to spray just a tiny amount of the rosy scent on a corner of a white handkerchief, shake it, fold it, and bury it in the pocket of her trousers.

Ready now, she opened her front door. Her unpainted face for the world to see; she was met by the briny scent of the river nearby. It was a glorious wintry day in Ashville. So clear, so bright that you thought it improved your eyesight.

Cocooned inside her black three-quarter-length quilted parka, Mrs. Brown began the walk to Mrs. Groton's house, leaving her cluttered neighborhood, where the houses were built right next to each other, then north along Main Street past the shops, town hall, and library, and across the Thompson Green, November gray and leafless but holding the promise of so much color come spring.

Here was the statue of Christopher Columbus the people of Ashville were so proud of. Mrs. Brown always liked to stop and read the poem inscribed on it.

"Brave Admiral, say but one good word:
What shall we do when hope is gone?"
The words leapt like a leaping sword:
"Sail on! Sail on! Sail on! And on!"

. . . .

He gained a world; he gave that world
Its grandest lesson: "On! Sail on!"

Mrs. Brown walked. Crossing Broad Street, she arrived at another green, Franklin Green, named for Benjamin Franklin, surrounded by the finest eighteenth- and nineteenth-century houses in Ashville, including, especially, Mrs. Groton's, the largest, and the prettiest of them all.

Mrs. Brown, who would have hated to arrive late, was instead half an hour early. She wasn't quite sure what to do next.

She sat on a bench next to a Revolutionary War cannon. From this perch Mrs. Brown regarded Mrs. Groton's house with great satisfaction, civic pride. After six decades of admiring it, within a matter of minutes she'd be inside.

Although she did not have the benefit of knowing the architectural terms to describe the house, here is what you saw when you looked across Franklin Green: a white clapboard Victorian Italianate villa built in the 1860s, with lavish details, spiraled twisted columns and capitals of the Composite order (a combination of the Ionic and the Corinthian), arched double front doors, molded shelves above the shuttered first-floor windows, and pointed pediments crowning the second-floor windows. It was five bays wide, very spacious, with a wing to the left of the façade that contained a ballroom and butler's pantry, which had been added when Mrs. Groton's great-great-grandmother married a Cabot from Boston. The society wedding was one for the history books.

At 9:25, five minutes before she was expected, at 9:30 A.M., Mrs. Brown walked across Franklin Green and, holding her breath, unlatched the gate of the ornate wrought-iron fence, went in, and climbed the three steps onto the entrance porch.

She rang the brass doorbell at the right of the arched double front doors. Mrs. Brown could hear the bell ringing inside the house. It seemed an eternity, but in fact was really just a matter of seconds, and the door opened.

Standing on the other side was a young woman the likes of which Mrs. Brown had never seen, at least not in person. Yes, in the fashion magazines she might look at when business was slow at the beauty parlor, and in the movies back in the day of Grace Kelly. The woman answering the door was tall and blond, skin the color of vanilla ice cream. She towered, and confidently, in impossibly high heels, and was dressed in a lightweight black cashmere turtleneck and a black pencil skirt to the knee with a slight, but decided, flounce behind.

The seamstress in Mrs. Brown was riveted by the well-sewn constraint of this tailored flounce and observed it closely when the young woman turned and walked back into the house, telling her to follow.

"So rude of me not to introduce myself at the door, but it is cold out there today, it is much warmer in the city," the young woman said, extending her delicate hand to Mrs. Brown. The heavy link bracelet of a large gold watch brushed cold on Mrs. Brown's wrist.

"My name is Rachel Ames and I was Mrs. Groton's assistant until her death and you must be . . ."

God help us, Rachel thought. Who is this

slender, little tobacco-gray wren of a sixty-something-year-old woman shaking nervously in the foyer of the great house? She thought she must be the cleaning lady, except she'd met the cleaning lady and this wasn't the woman, was it?

Her day was hectic, and overwhelming. The pressure had been mounting ever since Delphine Staunton, the expert from Lambton's, the posh international auction house, had arrived to conduct the Groton inventory. You know the type? They are arch and ornery, mistrusting, always challenging the authenticity of everything and everyone in the name of getting provenance right. Maybe their jobs depend on such relentless expertise, but it makes them seem sometimes like such snobs.

"Ah, yes," Rachel said aloud, realizing who this was. "The lady from the thrift shop. Thank you for coming, there is so much for us to do today. May I take your coat, Mrs. . . . ?"

"Brown," Mrs. Brown answered. "Mrs. Brown, but I'm not the lady you mean from the thrift shop . . ."

"You aren't the lady from the thrift shop? Then who are you?" Rachel asked. She was worried she had allowed a stranger into the house.

"I mean," Mrs. Brown said, her voice quivering.

She was astounded. First by the palatial foyer she found herself in. Then there was the sweeping staircase. All the way up to the second floor the walls were covered in heavy-framed paintings of people as historic looking as the portraits you find on currency.

"Yes, Mrs. Brown?" Rachel said, crossing her arms over her chest.

"I'm just here to help Mrs. Wood; she's the one you will want to be talking to from the thrift shop; she runs the place. Mrs. Wood isn't here yet?"

Rachel smiled kindly, the way well-brought-up people used to and some still do. Rachel intuited Mrs. Brown's nervousness as appreciation for the great house.

"Did you know Mrs. Groton, Mrs. Brown?" she asked, walking deeper into the foyer.

Mrs. Brown followed. She had never seen anything as dazzling as this house. It was stunning, in every sense.

"Mrs. Brown?"

"Ma'am?"

"I wonder, did you know Mrs. Groton?"

Rachel paused in front of a large ancestral portrait of an elegant older lady. She was majestically elongated, her white hair piled softly on her head. She wore a cream-colored chiffon tea dress to the ground. Her hands held three long-stemmed white roses. The woman's eyes were porcelain blue, but melancholy. Their gaze locked with yours.

"I didn't know Mrs. Groton personally, no, ma'am, of course I didn't," Mrs. Brown said. "Except every summer during the Rose Festival I always made it to the front of the line to watch her walk from this house over to the tent on opening day."

Rachel listened.

"She was so clean, Miss Ames, I don't think I've ever seen anyone who was so clean. Or so comfortable in her own skin, and so well put together."

Rachel smiled.

"Who's that, if I may ask?" Mrs. Brown pointed to the portrait.

Rachel explained that it was Mrs. Groton's grandmother painted by an artist named Boldini in 1923. It soon would be hanging at the Metropolitan Museum of Art on Fifth Avenue.

Rachel entered the dining room. It was as big as a restaurant, with a long mahogany table and twenty-four chairs. French doors opened to Mrs. Groton's topiary and rose gardens.

40

Standing by the doors, holding a clipboard, was a woman Mrs. Brown found terrifying looking. With a helmet of raven-black hair, here was the aforementioned auction house expert Delphine Staunton.

"As I was saying, Rachel," Delphine said, with an accent Mrs. Brown could not place, "every woman should be pretty in her own dining room. This is a very French idea," which she pronounced as "eye-dee," one that, "my people being French, of course, I agree with. The quality of this furniture, Philadelphia Chippendale, will command huge sales for us, I mean, for the estate, but this, how do you say, WASP decorating, is not very feminine, no? It is too stark, too plain. I doubt Mrs. Groton's looks were ever flattered here in this room."

Delphine shook her head disapprovingly. "It's not a room that flatters a woman. *Quel dommage,* don't you think? No wonder she preferred the Westchester place. She would have looked better in her dining room there, the glossy green walls, the red silk chairs."

As the raven-headed auctioneer opined, she crisscrossed the dining room sticking little green dots on the furniture. Or white dots, or no dots. Green meant it was going to Lambton's to be auctioned, white for the pieces of furniture and art bequeathed to

41

museums — the Boldini, for instance, and a jolly New York City street scene by the American impressionist painter Childe Hassam — and everything else, from the copper pots and utensils in the kitchen to the majority of Mrs. Groton's clothes, would be given to the thrift shop, hence Mrs. Brown's and Mrs. Wood's presence, if Mrs. Wood ever bothered to show up. How in the world could she possibly be late today of all days?

"Delphine Staunton, from Lambton's auction house, in New York, this is Mrs. Brown from the Ashville Thrift Shop," Rachel said, introducing the two women.

"Hello," Mrs. Brown said, her voice echoing in the large dining room.

Ms. Staunton didn't even bother to look. She twinkled her fingers, a kind of wave, in Mrs. Brown's general direction.

"People are going to think your little thrift shop is an outpost of Bergdorf Goodman," Delphine said, placing green dots on the rococo porcelain chickens decorating the mantel on the dining room's marble fireplace. "I'd wager never has such finery been sent your way, Mrs. Brown, never, ever."

Delphine was not looking at her when she said this, but was now bending over to inspect a brass bucket holding chopped wood.

Mrs. Brown had encountered women like this in the beauty parlor. Whether their remarks were intended to hurt, and so often they did, Mrs. Brown knew the best thing to do was to not respond, take the high road, and let her silence get loud enough that the offender either desisted, apologized, or changed the subject.

The doorbell rang, its echo deep — "very high church" is how the Episcopal bishop of Rhode Island had always described the sound of Mrs. Groton's bell.

Rachel excused herself.

Mrs. Brown hoped it was Mrs. Wood from the thrift shop. She was left alone with Delphine, now on her knees inspecting the marble fireplace. Then, rising, she turned her shellacked black head and looked Mrs. Brown up and down.

"Did you get your outfit at your thrift shop? Don't you wonder who wore it before you? We auction wonderful vintage pieces, maintained and dry-cleaned by experts before they are sold, but I couldn't wear secondhand clothes myself, you know? I would feel like I was wearing a ghost, let alone my phobia about catching bedbugs," Delphine said.

She squinted in Mrs. Brown's direction. "Have you ever had bedbugs in Ashville?

Les punaises de lit, en français, which sounds much better, *non?*"

Delphine exited the dining room for the pantry. With a whoosh, the door closed behind her.

Mrs. Brown did not respond, nor did she follow in some misguided need to be helpful. She took a breath; she exhaled. Through the French doors she could see the bones of Mrs. Groton's garden outside. The garden must be so beautiful when it is in bloom, she thought.

A few moments later, she heard Rachel and Delphine talking in the pantry. There was still no sign of Mrs. Wood, even though the doorbell had just rung.

"I don't like that woman," Delphine said. "I had a visceral dislike. It was instant."

"To whom? Certainly not poor Mrs. Brown?"

"Yes, Mrs. Brown," Delphine answered.

"But why? She's so dear."

"She's too plain. I never trust that," Delphine said.

"Be careful, Delphine, please," Rachel said. "She might hear you."

Mrs. Brown had heard. Of course it hurt. But she wasn't going to let it ruin the delight of being in the remarkable house of Millicent Groton. Besides, Mrs. Brown

44

knew she was plain. She knew it would be pure folly ever to try to prove that she wasn't, nor did she want to. And if it made this poorly behaved New York–dwelling Frenchwoman feel better to deprecate Mrs. Brown, so be it.

She'd turn the other cheek, because, thank God, she could.

"Oh, Emilia, I am so sorry not to have gotten here earlier," Margaret Wood said, bustling and fluttering into the dining room.

Margaret Wood was a short woman with a very large frame and full bosom hardly concealed under the cotton pink pullover sweater she was wearing with a midi-length black corduroy skirt. It drooped above her ankles and her white tennis shoes. Her hair was blond as a dandelion, and her face was lined with wrinkles and tan from the summer, and the many summers before.

"Have you ever?"

"Ever what?"

"Ever seen a house as grand as this?" Margaret Wood asked, whispering, although they were alone.

Mrs. Brown and Mrs. Wood shook their heads in disbelief. They most certainly had never seen a house like this before or could they ever expect to again.

CHAPTER 4

"Then what happened?" Alice asked.

Keeping to their nearly every-evening ritual, they sat at Mrs. Brown's ancient, green and blue oilcloth-covered kitchen table discussing their day. Tonight they were trying a new tea called Hu-Kwa. Rachel had given Mrs. Brown an unopened tin of it.

The tea, Mrs. Groton's favorite — there were several more tins left in the pantry of the great house — had a stocky, smoky taste that took some getting used to. Alice was about to say, but managed not to before it slipped out of her mouth, that the tea smelt like old rubber.

"It's not only beautiful, the house is so peaceful and so clean and so orderly," Mrs. Brown said. "I can't explain it. What it meant to me to see things so . . . so perfectly arranged."

Mrs. Brown wasn't going to mention Delphine Staunton's nastiness. She never

46

thought it wise for anyone to look too long at the negative things in her life. Where you look, there you go.

From across the street came the sound of their neighbors, a young married couple arguing — again. They tried not to notice.

Mrs. Brown moved a plate of her home-made oatmeal shortbread closer to Alice. This got the cat's attention, and Santo leapt from his owner's lap onto the table. He was removed to the floor immediately.

"The dining room alone was as big as four of the houses on this street," Mrs. Brown continued. "There were so many beautiful things. There was even a silver mustard pot, that's what the lady from the auction house called it, a mustard pot, a tiny thing that she expected would be auctioned in New York City for . . . well, guess for how much?"

Alice liked a quiz and could be quite competitive, hating to get anything wrong. She calculated before she wagered her guess. "Five hundred dollars," she said.

"Twelve to fifteen thousand dollars, can you believe it?" Mrs. Brown exclaimed, sitting back in her chair. Santo returned to her lap.

"That must have been some very strong mustard in that pot," Alice said.

"There's an entire room, another big

47

room, they called the library, and I thought of your grandmother, how much Sarah would love this room. It is deep red wallpaper and curtains and towering bookcases and library steps and busts of — now let me see, because I promised I would try to remember for when I write your grandmother — of Shakespeare and I think they said Baron?"

"Byron?"

"That's right. That's what they said. Oh, good for you, Alice, and your grandmother always worries that you don't read; Byron, and all men, you know, not one woman, not even your grandmother's Jane."

Jane Austen being Mrs. Fox's favorite author.

"Go on, tell me more," Alice said, pouring more tea. Funny smell or not, she was getting used to the heady taste.

"There was this large wood desk. There were bound atlases, and soft chairs with reading lamps next to them, and a long table covered with piles of books, more busts, and photographs in silver frames. On the walls were framed paintings of horses and dogs . . . it was a remarkable room that you felt smarter just for walking into. They said it was Mr. Groton's study."

In England, and in America, too, until

World War II, if a gentleman didn't have a decent study then he wasn't considered a gentleman.

"And a fireplace, a beautiful marble fireplace with a sofa in front of it," Mrs. Brown said. "You could spend the rest of your life there, Alice, and be very happy, I think."

Alice smiled. Could she really be content living in what sounded like a museum? "Yes, it sounds like I'd be very happy there," she said to be polite and supportive.

"Who wouldn't be?" Mrs. Brown said. Then she reconsidered. "I suppose an unhappy person wouldn't be happy there . . ."

"After the novelty wore off," Alice said, finishing Mrs. Brown's sentence. "For people who feel that something's always missing wherever they're at, the void becomes an abyss in a bigger place."

"Does it?" Mrs. Brown asked.

"Absolutely. In every fairy tale I've ever read," Alice said, biting into a piece of shortbread, "and I've read them all. When I was a kid, I mean."

You're still a kid, Mrs. Brown almost said, but didn't. Leaving some things unsaid is an underestimated virtue. Doing so was a credo that Mrs. Brown survived by.

CHAPTER 5

"If that nasty piece of work says one more time, 'This or that isn't good enough for Lambton's but it'll be like a piece of Tiffany for your little thrift shop,' I think I will scream," Mrs. Wood was saying, her face pink with rage.

She and Mrs. Brown met on Franklin Green the next morning so they could arrive together at Mrs. Groton's.

Rachel was dressed today in a beige pencil skirt to her knees, a white oxford shirt crisply folded below her elbows, brown alligator shoes with a sturdy four-inch heel. She welcomed the Ashville locals with coffee, tea, morning glory muffins, and donuts in the kitchen.

Just as the women settled around Mrs. Groton's kitchen table to sip and chat before pressing on with the inventory taking, Delphine Staunton, wearing a waist-length red-black kimono sort of bed jacket

over black pants and shirt, entered complaining.

"I'm so exhausted," she said.

Delphine readjusted the black cashmere
sweater she'd tied over the waist of her black
trousers.

"That inn may be centuries-old charm,
but the walls are so thin I heard everything
from every room last night. I mean I could
even hear one of those dreadful housewives'
shows on the television in the next room!
Then I stayed awake worrying about *les punaises de lit.* Bloody hell!"

Delphine stared at the baked goods on the
kitchen table as if they were frosted with
punaises.

"Gluten?" she asked, looking Mrs. Wood
up and down.

"Oh, Delphine, how awful," Rachel said.
"Why don't you stay here in the house
tonight?"

Delphine smiled coldly. "Thanks, but I
think I can finish up today by seven or eight
and then I will drive back to New York.
Most everything in the upstairs rooms is
better left in the upstairs rooms, lovely,
charming, what you would expect in a
weekend house like this, but not valuable
enough for Lambton's, so you can have all
of it for the thrift shop. Or give it to the

homeless. Have you many homeless here in Ashville?"

Mrs. Wood bit as far as she could into a cheese Danish to keep herself quiet.

"The drive back to town is more than four hours," Rachel said. "If you are exhausted it might be too much, too dangerous."

"Oh, I will be fine once I get into my groove here this morning," Ms. Staunton said, pouring herself a cup of black coffee. "By the way, I wonder what you think of this idea, Rachel. I was speaking on the phone last night with one of my colleagues, and the current thinking for the auction catalogue cover image is to use the photograph of Millicent" — Delphine was the only person calling Mrs. Groton by her first name — "chatting with the Queen taken at the wedding of Marie-Chantal Miller to Pavlos of Greece. It is a beautiful photograph, the old gals look divine — love those huge hats they're wearing — but my colleagues are split on whether it is a good idea or not . . ."

Delphine took a deep breath. She walked across the kitchen, looked dramatically toward the garden, rested her right hand on her right hip, turned back to Rachel, said:

"I think the Queen is history."

"History, Delphine?"

Delphine explained. "Don't get me wrong, I'm French. We like monarchs, with or without their heads."

Delphine checked her phone for e-mails and texts, but continued talking. "Although personally, except for the furnishings, I think Versailles was overrated."

Delphine was highly caffeinated this morning. "But I appreciate that there is great value for British tourism in having a monarchy. It's all about branding. America has baseball and Las Vegas to drive tourism and England has Buckingham Palace, all great show and ritual — genius branding."

She continued: "It's just that in this difficult economy we have to really, really work to market the auction to as many high-end consumers as possible, and when it comes to the top one percent, the new money made in tech and digital — I daresay most of the new, big Wall Street money as well — my colleagues and I don't think they will give a good goddamn about the Queen or any royalty. The only royalty they are interested in is rock-and-roll royalty, you know?"

Rachel looked puzzled.

Delphine shrugged. "We must avoid giving the appearance that Mrs. Groton's antiques are old, if you see what I mean."

No one did.

Delphine continued. "If we put a photo of Millicent, say, with Bill and Melinda Gates on the cover of the catalogue, and there is one we can get permission to use, taken at Warren Buffett's birthday a few years ago, we can better make the point that anything you buy at Lambton's, even when in the millions and millions of dollars, isn't shopping for antiques, it is environmental, recycling at the highest level. And therefore all about doing something really, really important for the environment; they love this kind of crap thinking in Silicon Valley. *C'est très* Yahoo."

Delphine poured herself another cup of hot coffee. Apparently no longer averse to gluten, she pinched a bit of buttery crust off a cheese Danish and dropped it in her open mouth.

As it happened, Mrs. Wood was devoted to the Queen of England. She was a veritable repository of historical information and popular trivia about Her Majesty.

One of her favorite tidbits? The first time Princess Elizabeth fully realized she had ascended to the role of Queen was when milk bottles arrived from the royal dairy with the crest "EIIR" on them.

Delphine's dismissal of the Queen infuriated Mrs. Wood.

Rachel had many thoughts and responses to what Delphine was saying. Sensing the anger brewing in Margaret Wood, she felt it important to proceed diplomatically.

"The cover of the catalogue is very important, isn't it?" Rachel asked.

She knew it was but wanted to soothe Delphine. Poor thing hadn't slept well.

"Oh, yes, it's huge," Delphine said. "*Huge!* The cover of the catalogue is also the image used in all the advertising and the press materials — branding. And I don't think the Queen is relevant."

"Perhaps we should consult with the executors of the estate," Rachel said. "They are charged with the responsibility of making sure they attain as much profit as possible for all the charities that will benefit from the auction of Mrs. Groton's things."

"Well, I for one think the Queen is passé. Queen out; Gateses in. Or Jay Z and Beyoncé! They're really the new Mr. and Mrs. Astor in New York. Do you think any such photo exists?"

Rachel saw the pained expressions on Mrs. Wood's and Mrs. Brown's faces.

"I don't know, Delphine," Rachel said thoughtfully. "You know, when the sad day comes and the Queen dies? I wonder if the world is prepared. Do we have any idea, any clue at all, of what will go with her?"

"A few corgis, and a case of gin?"

Mrs. Wood wasn't amused. "I think the Queen is better than Mother Teresa even!" Mrs. Wood said.

Delphine Staunton shrugged.

Rachel continued. "No, really, Delphine, think about everything she represents: decorum, civility, constraint, consistency, endurance, duty, service, faith, hope . . . and deriving satisfaction from living for these principles. Rather than a life trying to satisfy personal wants and entitlements, as the majority of us do, and are encouraged to do, all in the name of success."

Rachel was on a roll. "We do not have any enduring figures, any archetypes, who represent kindness and courtesy, the way England has the Queen. Whom do we have? Our presidents and other elected officials aren't principled because they are political, always dancing around for votes. The only constants we have are tycoons and movie stars, and their positions are hardly fixed. Every culture needs its constants. We've had to borrow the Queen. Americans probably need the Queen more than her own people do."

Delphine shrugged again, made a little pucker with her lips, indicating she dismissed the conversation. This only fueled Rachel to continue.

"I can think of very few in public life today, except maybe Caroline Kennedy, who have survived disappointments and sadness — not to mention endless scrutiny — with so much grace. Here's a woman who has lost a king and a queen, who also happened to be her parents; her sister; her uncle, who was blown up in a terrorist attack . . ." She paused.

"I could go on, but I'll stop." Rachel sighed. "All I am trying to say is, about Queen Elizabeth, we live in a world where we only know what we've got when it's gone. And that's a damn shame."

"Sorry, Rachel, who knew you felt this way? Been dating an Englishman lately? Thanks to globalization, I hear they aren't as bad in bed as they supposedly used to be." Delphine laughed.

Rachel was ice cold, a temperature swans excel in.

"I think I'd better get to work here before you ladies deliver me to the Tower of London for my beheading," Delphine said, and left the kitchen.

CHAPTER 6

Mrs. Brown was dispatched to Mrs. Groton's bedroom and dressing room upstairs.

Here was yet another revelation to behold in this magical residence: a blue and white canopied king-size bed, a sitting room–office, and a large dressing room that was wall to wall, floor to ceiling, closets and shelves. In the center was a sitting area with two matching rose-pattern-chintz-covered chairs and a sofa.

Mrs. Wood was downstairs taking inventory of the things Delphine deemed unworthy for high auction.

"Ashville, Ashville, Ashville," the auctioneer kept repeating as if she was counting odorous fish.

Mrs. Brown's task, meanwhile, was to go through the various drawers and closets and count the trousers, tops, shoes, scarves, handkerchiefs, sunglasses, and more items that would be sent to the Ashville Thrift Shop.

The quantity, as well as the quality, of, say, the twenty-seven cotton-knit short-sleeved golfing shirts in various colors bemused her, as did a row of seven pairs of identical white cotton summer trousers. Fortunately, envy was not in Mrs. Brown's nature. Even when she came upon a red cardigan sweater with a lush chinchilla collar, she felt only pure delight.

Mrs. Brown opened drawers — many filled with rose-scented or evergreen-scented sachets — counted items, and scribbled the tally on sheet after sheet of yellow legal paper. When she finished with the sweaters and lingerie in all the drawers, Mrs. Brown moved on to the closets.

The first closet she opened was empty, except for about a dozen fine wood clothing hangers. Rachel had said earlier that Mrs. Groton kept only a few dressy things in Ashville. These Mrs. Brown found in the next closet.

Two dresses: one was an orange-yellow floral silk caftan-style evening dress with bell-shaped long sleeves and a V-neck. But as beautiful as it was, the confection did not capture Mrs. Brown's attention as much as the other dress did. This was a sleeveless black dress and a single-button jacket made of the finest quality wool crepe.

Its correctness was its allure. Suggesting endless possibilities and the certainty of positive outcomes if one wore this dress. The richness of the affect of this suit, its elegance and poise, was the work of a master.

It was the strangest thing, but even in her youth, never had a dress, or any other item of clothing, spoken to Mrs. Brown this way, a garment so regal — so "grown-up" she'd later explain in one of her letters to Mrs. Fox — so exquisitely tailored and, somehow, thoroughly reassuring.

Why wasn't all of life designed so perfectly?

Lest there be any confusion, this was no "little black dress." It was not a sibling in the family of frocks you see trotted out on fashion pages at least once a year, a cotillion of easy-breezy, channel-your-inner–Audrey Hepburn black shift dresses to wear from desk to dinner.

It was the queen of all little black dresses, the jewel in the crown. Mrs. Brown fell under its spell.

Reaching out to touch the dress, she stopped. Seeing how roughened and red her hands were from cleaning and housework, and aghast at the sight, she pulled them back.

Rachel, carrying a small pile of books, saw this.

"Isn't that a wonderful dress? You'd never know, would you, that it is more than twenty years old; there's not a thread out of place," she said as she entered the dressing room from the hall.

"The style is one of Oscar de la Renta's most popular. He always has it, or something very much like it, every season. In fact, it's a style almost every First Lady in the past thirty years has owned."

Mrs. Brown recalled seeing photographs in the magazines at the beauty parlor of Hillary Clinton and Laura Bush, a Democrat and a Republican, in what she now realized was this dress, or a close version of it. In Mrs. Brown's opinion, First Ladies, even Jackie Kennedy, were their most attractive not looking like butterfly duchesses in their evening dresses but in these elegant day dresses and skirt suits that said they meant business and that they got things done.

Mrs. Brown's ideal dress — this dress — was the complete opposite of Cinderella's. Cinderella wanted to go to the grand dance in a ball gown; Mrs. Brown's dream was this dress: suitability in every sense.

It's a great fault of the current fashion system that rather than innovating on the functionality of what we wear, the industry mostly only addresses the fear of not looking young, trendy, or rich. And when it comes to new clothes that women with less than upper-middle-class incomes — women like Mrs. Brown and her peers — can afford, fashion fails and discriminates most. Unless mature women want to wear the same things that twenty-six-year-olds covet, there's very little that's happily intended for them to wear. And the exquisite enhancements of luxury tailoring? Out of reach.

Not every woman wants to look like her teenage daughter or granddaughter. Not every woman wants to look better suited for partying in Las Vegas than for holding steadfast at home and at work. Not every woman's fantasy is to walk a red carpet. Not every woman feels obliged to wear the latest trend just for trends' sake.

Rachel could not read the actual thoughts telegraphing in her mind but, with her feminine intuition, understood that something quite major was occurring today in the heart of the Ashville lady.

From her female relations, or reading the memoirs of dynamic women throughout history, Rachel was attuned to the fact that at any given stage over the course of a lifetime, a woman thinks, and feels, differently about what she wears.

In the beginning, when she is young, fashion is fast currency, a way of communicating, signaling; an aphrodisiac, whether it is motorcycle leather pants or dotted swiss lacy blouses, something, like feathers, to attract the mate who will parent your children, fill your nest, perpetuate a glittering species. Got to have it!

In the middle years, it is not so much feathers as it is futures that you reflect in clothing, your prosperity and abundance. Later, the hope of clothing is self-preservation, protection from the eliminations of time fraying life, gravity undoing your hem.

It is style over sorrow.

What you wear is your container. It circumvents the chaos and the disappointments; structure holds you, it coddles, it corsets. Fashion becomes an intervention now. The application of lipstick when one is ill to make one feel better. And by doing something so seemingly superficial you console and inspire the people around you, who care and are so worried. You powder your face. You wear your best shoes. You button your jacket. You smooth the folds in your skirt.

Wanting to relieve Mrs. Brown of any

embarrassment from having just been observed, with her hand quite literally in Mrs. Groton's closet, Rachel sped her conversation into a jolly kind of privileged singsong, something she'd learned from watching Mrs. Groton: in any potentially awkward situation, employ levity and self-deprecating humor to make people feel their best.

"How embarrassing! Look at me with all these old books. They look pretty interesting, so I thought I'd bring them with me to the city. I always read before I go to sleep," Rachel said, resting half a dozen books on a dressing table. "I promise, I'll send them right back to you at the thrift shop to sell."

The pile included paperback mystery novels and biographies. But it was a teaberry-colored hardback that intrigued Mrs. Brown.

"Looks like fun, doesn't it?" Rachel said, handing the book to Mrs. Brown. "Do you like to read, Mrs. Brown?"

The cover was an illustration of a sweet-looking lady in a tan twill coat and a green straw hat with a large pink rose pinned to it.

"I do like to read," Mrs. Brown said. "What's this one about?"

Rachel read the title aloud. "*Mrs. 'Arris Goes to Paris,* by Paul Gallico. Hmm, I don't know, looks like a kids' book for grown-ups, but the fact that the lady on the cover is carrying a Dior dress box certainly is a recommendation — to me at least. Why don't you take it?"

"I couldn't take anything from here," Mrs. Brown said.

"Nor could I," said Rachel, "except a book. You know, Mrs. Groton forgave everyone almost anything if they were readers. Please take the book, Mrs. Brown, and enjoy it. Consider it a loan that never needs to be repaid, or sell it at the thrift shop after you've read it, if that makes you feel easier about taking it."

Mrs. Brown hesitated.

"Besides," Rachel continued, "I think Mrs. Groton would have liked you very much and been pleased to know you had something of hers from her house in Ashville."

Hearing that Mrs. Groton would have liked her, had they ever met, gave Mrs. Brown a feeling of pride that pulled her right up, posture perfect. She was very pleased but still not comfortable accepting a present, especially under the circumstances. She was here to help inventory the deceased woman's most personal effects. Wasn't it ghoulish to take something?

But Rachel insisted. Mrs. Brown remembered what her mother always told her. If you are offered a glass of water in someone's home, always accept it, whether you are thirsty or not. This shows that you visit with pleasure, not resistance.

Mrs. Brown thanked Rachel for her kindness and accepted the book, taking delight in just holding it.

But now back to work.

Concerning the two dresses in the closet, the flowing floral evening dress and the Oscar de la Renta suit, Rachel said: "Both dresses are to be packed in tissue, by me before I am done here this week, and brought to New York, where they will, along with many other things from Mrs. Groton's closets, go to the Costume Institute at the Metropolitan Museum."

Rachel touched the sleeve of the flowery dress. "Mrs. Groton was on all the best-dressed lists, and much of her clothing, excuse me, all of her clothing in various special ways, was exceptional and some pieces very important."

"Important?" Mrs. Brown wondered.

"Meaning, they were significant pieces in the various designers' careers. This evening dress dates back to the late 1970s and was designed by Giorgio di Sant' Angelo. It was the lead dress in the collection that got him his first Coty Award. So the Met considers it 'important.' "

Mrs. Brown didn't know how to respond.

"Modern women want choices to go with their moods," Rachel continued. "But since most modern women's mood is perpetual exhaustion, I think the trickle down is the preponderance of casual jogging suits, jeans, and T-shirts that you see women wearing everywhere, airports, grocery stores, picking the kids up at school."

Rachel paused.

"People dress for comfort, not for occasion or suitability. I went to a funeral the other day of someone who worked for Mrs. Groton at her house in Westchester, and no one dressed up, you know, that one sovereign outfit people used to have for significant occasions," Rachel said.

"Except for those wonderful ladies in the South, does anyone dress for church anymore?" Rachel laughed. "I guess the question tells you where I am not on Sundays. Oh, dear. More praying and less bloviating for me!"

Mrs. Brown was quiet.

"Mrs. Groton's advice for older women who want to look good was to dress to look important, not sexy. And by 'important'

Mrs. Groton meant to look grown-up, a ready and easy-to-identify asset that bettered one's family and community. What you wear? It not only protects you but projects the best person you want to be, and helps get you to that place."

Rachel worried she might have hurt Mrs. Brown's feelings.

"Just between us," Rachel confided, "Mrs. Groton didn't wake up every morning of her life, especially after her son died, feeling like 'Mrs. Groton.' Many mornings she woke up in a cloud of depression. One of the best ways she knew to move that dark cloud from hanging over her was to, as she said, 'suit up and show up.' Or 'put on my war paint.' The war was her depression and the paint was her makeup and hair."

A warrior's outfit; Mrs. Brown touched the right sleeve of the black suit dress.

"As I was saying before I digressed, about the Oscar de la Renta here going to the Met? The dress is important for curatorial purposes for several reasons," Rachel said. "For the designer, it represents one of his most classic and popular designs. Furthermore, it's significant to the Met because it's what Mrs. Groton wore to luncheon with the Queen — we were talking about the Queen earlier — at Buckingham Palace ten years ago. And it is what she wore to the White House to lunch with the President and First Lady. Along with the Sant' Angelo, she eventually retired the dress here to Ashville because her closets in New York were getting too full."

Rachel took the dress from the closet and held it closer for inspection. "It is the finest wool crepe sheath, with a bit of stretch, very sturdy but also very lithe. I like the square neck, cap sleeve; the jacket, the notch collar. It's genius, isn't it?"

Genius? Mrs. Brown wondered. She'd never heard anyone less than a scientist — let alone a dress — described this way. Later, she would come to understand that "genius" is fashion-speak for "I like it."

"It's also genius that the jacket has just one button, because you see how it helps the jacket minimize any stomach by providing a sort of bell-shape effect," Rachel continued.

Mrs. Brown studied the jacket closely.

"This one button is beautiful, isn't it? It's real tortoise-shell, belonging to Mrs. Groton long before the hawksbill sea turtle was classified an endangered species. Mrs. Groton first had it on an Yves Saint Laurent couture 'le smoking,' as the French say, or tuxedo, as we say, that she had from the

69

1960s, when she was still buying haute couture."

The polished, Continental way Rachel pronounced "haute couture" was so elegant, it was like a trip to Paris itself. "Haute couture," she repeated. "It literally means 'high fashion' or 'finest high-fashion sewing' and refers to the made-to-order clothing the French design houses are so proud of and so good at."

Mrs. Brown knew the word. One did if one had learned sewing back in the 1950s using Vogue patterns to make one's clothes, and most did because they weren't expensive but they were chic. Her prom dress was from a Vogue pattern, a floral number with a full skirt that Mrs. Brown was able to make for just seventeen dollars, the cost of the fabric and buttons. Her mother made her wedding dress, from another Vogue pattern, for just over twenty-five dollars.

"May I?" she asked, indicating that she wanted to examine the dress more closely.

"Of course," Rachel answered.

Mrs. Brown carefully examined the hand-stitched lining of the skirt and the jacket. Just the way the silk fit so smoothly, without a hint of bunching under the arm, showed how superb the craftsmanship was. And was she correct? The lining wasn't black like the suit but a deep midnight navy blue?

"The lining is really impressive, isn't it?" Rachel said.

"Is it navy blue, not black?" Mrs. Brown asked.

"So genius, isn't it? Mrs. Groton said that when you get older you can line your dark suits in navy silk and it will cast a warm glow on your face, much less harsh than if it were black."

Nearly invisible piped patching on the pockets hid the topstitching that set them on the jacket, and the pockets were lined in the navy blue silk.

"Impressive stitching, isn't it?" Rachel said.

Mrs. Brown nodded. "How do you know so much about clothes?" she asked Rachel.

"Well, I love fashion, not only the clothes but the whole business of it and the people who work in the fashion industry. I went to Parsons School of Design and might have gone directly to Seventh Avenue had the opportunity to become Mrs. Groton's assistant not presented itself," she explained.

From the expression on Mrs. Brown's face, and her fascination with this garment, Rachel could tell that the older woman, despite her plainness, wasn't allergic to fashion either. In fact, she was falling in love with the dress.

Hasn't every woman fallen in love with a dress?

Rachel certainly had, and on many occasions. But it surprised Rachel that it was this suit dress and not the flowery, elegant evening dress next to it that had captured Mrs. Brown's heart. She wanted to know why, but good manners prevented her from asking personal questions of someone she had just met, especially this dear older woman from a different era and walk of life.

Perhaps if she talked about herself, however, Mrs. Brown would reveal more?

"The one thing lacking in my fashion knowledge is knowing how to sew, I mean really sew well," Rachel said. "I can manage a hem and stitch together a small tear. I understand construction intellectually, and I'm aware of a great many of the tricks a good tailor can do to create proportions that flatter. But if I had to actually make a dress, I don't think I could."

Rachel paused. "It would be hubris to say I'm a fashion expert. Rather like someone calling herself a foodie when she only really knows the basics of cooking but is very good ordering at fancy restaurants."

Mrs. Brown smiled. "Women my age all had to learn how to sew, and make their own clothes. For something special, we'd use patterns we'd buy at the five-and-dime. My mother taught me," she said. "I've been making my own clothes, as well as mending other people's to make extra money, since I was a teenager."

There was a drawer full of handkerchiefs that Mrs. Brown hadn't gotten to yet. Rachel helped her count them, a series of faded cotton handkerchiefs with pastel floral prints or green shamrocks. They were beautiful.

Mrs. Brown noticed the tears in Rachel's eyes.

"I miss Mrs. Groton," Rachel said.

"Me too," Mrs. Brown said softly, then embarrassed, quickly added, "everyone in Ashville does."

Rachel sighed. "Well, onward and upward. I'm lucky I've got a great job to go to in the fashion business as soon as everything in Mrs. Groton's houses is sorted."

It was getting late.

"How much would a dress and jacket like this cost if someone wanted to buy a new one today?" Mrs. Brown asked.

"Alas, a hefty amount, Mrs. Brown. About seven thousand dollars, maybe a bit more."

Seven thousand dollars!

It was a huge amount, Mrs. Brown knew.

73

Nonetheless, born was the idea that, as soon as humanly possible, Mrs. Brown would have just such a dress and jacket hanging in her closet. Maybe if she did, it could set something right. Symbolically. Isn't every act of faith a symbol before it becomes a deed?

But how dare she? she wondered.

How dare she not?

Crystallizing in her mind was what she needed to do. Go to New York? Oh, good God, this would take bravery, she knew — nothing less than the valor of a Marine, nearly a military-style campaign, a grown-up woman's version of Capture the Flag with real stakes.

Money.

Couldn't she find some copied version of this dress for so much cheaper from one of the bargain brands and discount stores? Maybe, but it didn't matter, that wasn't the point for Mrs. Brown. Couldn't she make this outfit at home and spare herself the trouble? No, she could not. She wished she had the skills, but she just didn't. Even if she was handed the secret muslin pattern, or toile, this suit dress that so enchanted her was something she could never replicate herself. It was sewing at the highest level.

Somehow, some way, she'd save up for it

— even if it took the rest of her life.

And then, heaven help her, she'd go to New York, where she'd never been, which she was always afraid of, and buy the dress.

Of course she knew that people shopped for clothing online, even expensive clothing like this. But this required something more, discovery and expedition.

She'd find her way. She'd bring the dress home.

CHAPTER 7

It was suppertime before every last bit and remnant of Mrs. Groton's material life in Ashville was packed and accounted for.

There was a bitter wind and, if not rain, even the threat of snow.

Mrs. Brown walked home in the dark with the little novel that Rachel had given her tucked in her handbag. She thought she might mail it to Mrs. Fox to read first, or lend it to Alice, but decided that she would begin reading it tonight, and then pass it along if either of them would be interested to read it. She'd been as drawn to the book as she was to Mrs. Groton's perfect dress.

Mrs. Brown was in her kitchen less than five minutes, warming a serving of a ham and pea soup she had made over the weekend, good cat Santo positioned like a contented little Buddha on a kitchen chair, when there was a familiar tap on the door. Here was Alice.

"Have you eaten, Alice?" Mrs. Brown asked.

"Yes. It's late. I've finished grading my papers and I'm ready for some television and bed. You're home so late, late, I mean, for you. Where have you been? Are you okay?" Alice settled into her position at Mrs. Brown's table. She had been surprised earlier in the evening how worried she was when Mrs. Brown wasn't home yet.

Mrs. Brown made Alice a cup of the smoky tea that only yesterday Alice had said smelt like old rubber, but tonight it was ambrosia.

Heating up her supper, Mrs. Brown described the events of the day. She described how, as Rachel got sweeter and friendlier, Delphine Staunton had become haughtier.

"It's a stuck-up world, Mrs. Brown," Alice opined.

Was it always? Mrs. Brown wondered.

Mrs. Brown recounted in detail the contentious conversation about Queen Elizabeth.

"Rachel is right," Mrs. Brown said. "No one, especially the cynics, will know what is lost until she passes."

Alice had her doubts. She had no sense of the Queen of England except she was the grandmother-in-law of Kate Middleton, the

Duchess of Cambridge, whose wedding she had watched on television along with the rest of the world. She didn't admit this too often or too loudly, because she didn't think it too cool, but that royal wedding was amazing. And she sure wouldn't say no if it happened to her.

Alice changed her mind about not eating and joined Mrs. Brown in a cup of the pea soup and a piece of rye toast.

"Good stuff, Mrs. Brown."

"You like the soup, dear?" Mrs. Brown asked.

"Oh, yeah, the soup's good. But I meant your stories about Mrs. Groton's today. It's like an episode of Ashville's local *Downton Abbey* or *Upstairs, Downstairs,* except no one is upstairs anymore, with Mrs. Groton gone and all," Alice observed. "Unless you count that auction house lady, who doesn't sound like much of a lady, if you ask me."

Alice returned to her place across the way to watch some television before bed. She promised Mrs. Brown she'd drop by again tomorrow night for more conversation.

After Alice left, Mrs. Brown fed Santo his kibble and put water in his bowl. She washed the dishes and tidied the kitchen. By 9:30, in her white nightgown, she was ready for bed.

She knelt at the side of her bed, and thanked her God for keeping her faithful that day. That was always her prayer; nothing felt as bad in life as when she was lacking faith. She prayed for Mrs. Fox, and for Alice, who was such an unexpected new friend; for Bonnie at the beauty salon; for the neighbors across the street who fought; she prayed for Rachel's safe return to New York City, and Delphine Staunton's as well.

Once in bed, she opened her bedside table drawer and brought out the framed family photographs she kept out of sight during the day.

The photographs always gave her pause. The room crowded with memories.

Santo jumped on the bed and laid his head on top of the Paul Gallico novel she'd brought from Mrs. Groton's.

Mrs. Brown took the book from underneath the cat and opened it. Some four hours later, she had read over a third of the novel.

Set in the 1950s, *Mrs. 'Arris Goes to Paris* is the story of a London charwoman who happens upon an exquisitely beautiful and colorful haute couture Christian Dior long dress hanging in the closet of one of the sirens she cleans for. After the dark horrors, the sanctions, and the rationings of World

War II, the color and opulence of the silky gown is life changing to behold.

Although the dress that Mrs. Brown discovered in Mrs. Groton's closet was the complete opposite of the frilly, confectionery dress Mrs. 'Arris encounters, she identified with the character's longing for something transforming.

The dress that would change Mrs. Brown's life and motivate her soul was not chiffon froth and sparkling color. Hers was the dress of the subtle lady rather than the eternal siren. And it was an awakening, one that Mrs. Brown carried into her dreams that night and into morning the next day.

Of sweet dreams and schemes, Mrs. Brown promised herself that as soon as possible tomorrow she would come up with her plan for getting the dress.

CHAPTER 8

At six the next morning, her alarm went off. At the sound, Santo, asleep at the foot of her bed, jumped on her stomach. That woke her up for sure. Her two days in Mrs. Groton's wonderland were over. It was time to return to work, back of the house, as they say in showbiz, at Bonnie's Beauty Salon.

Santo led the way into the kitchen. Mrs. Brown filled her electric kettle with tap water for her tea, extra-strong this morning. She then returned to her bedroom and made her bed, put the treasured photographs back in their drawer, and with them went the cherished copy of Mrs. Groton's novel about the London charwoman. Despite not having had the long night's sleep she was typically accustomed to, Mrs. Brown was galvanized by a sense of purpose she hadn't felt in years.

She bathed quickly and, never fussing over what to wear, dressed in her standard mufti, gray pants and a brown sweater.

A piece of toast with a dab of butter and a spoonful of the orange marmalade she'd made before Christmas last year — her mother's recipe that mixed Seville and blood oranges — and she was out her door at 7:30, some thirty minutes later than usual. She had the key to the beauty parlor, and it was her job to get in first, open the place, make the coffee, and tidy up before the first beautician and customer arrived at eight.

It was just a twenty-minute walk to work, so Mrs. Brown had sold her car several years ago. Alice had the keys to Mrs. Fox's car if she needed to get anywhere, as Alice also had access to her grandmother's computer, not to mention her own laptop, if Mrs. Brown ever wanted to look something up, like a recipe, or buy something online, which she rarely did. She preferred shopping locally, not as an eco trend but because it was her custom.

As she went briskly toward Andover Street, the cold Ashville morning air was as bracing as it was familiar. Mrs. Brown was glad for the walk. It always did her good, except when there was heavy snow and ice and she had to be especially careful not to fall. She couldn't afford to lose work because of an injury.

Walking across Jefferson Street now and onto Main Street, she saw Bonnie's sandwiched between the Village Cheese Shop and the barbershop owned by Ashville's biggest gossip, Solomon Aquilino. Her mind was focused on the events of yesterday at Mrs. Groton's and keeping her promise to herself to figure out a plan for getting her dress. But how? When she got home tonight after work she would make a budget, somehow, some way, create a plan to earn and save enough money to buy that dress.

At Bonnie's, Mrs. Brown found that the white Cape Cod–style door to the beauty parlor was unlocked. Bonnie came in early to work when she couldn't sleep well (and could be nasty and ornery all day as a result).

Stepping inside this salon box of feminine self-preservation, where walls and furnishings were either white or turquoise, Mrs. Brown heard an unusual sound, moaning, almost a deep wailing. She cautiously inched inside and surveyed the space just in case there had been a break-in, not that there was a lot of crime in Ashville, but there were those unfortunate moments. Everything appeared in order: a salon with six workstations — sinks, parlor chairs, counters, and cupboards flanking the walls.

The puzzling sound Mrs. Brown heard was coming from Bonnie's office. She was worried. Maybe Bonnie Provost was a bit much at times, too self-involved, too dramatic, too New Age, but Mrs. Brown always wished her well; she was decent enough, most of the time. It would be awful if anything bad had happened to her.

You probably will not be surprised to know that Bonnie had great hair, as well as good skin — she'd stopped sunbathing in her early twenties, a dermatological godsend. Because of her sable-colored hair, glowing complexion, distinctive nose, excellent manicure, and feminine curves, she fancied herself a younger Barbra Streisand.

At the sound of another wail, Mrs. Brown rushed to Bonnie's office in the back of the salon, praying she wasn't having a heart attack or some other deadly convulsive disorder.

Mr. Brown had had a heart attack, and the memory of it flashed across her mind. Not for the first time, he'd come home drunk from the bar over on Washington Street. Mrs. Brown had struggled to get him into bed. She'd finally succeeded and, as she did on these nights, was sleeping on the sofa in the front room when she heard yelping and groaning from the bedroom.

She rushed to Mr. Brown and tried to help.

Seconds before the paramedics arrived, the ambulance waking up not just the neighbors but practically everyone on their side of town, her husband died in her embrace. In his eyes was a look of profound apology — and abject terror.

But Mrs. Brown stopped before she reached Bonnie's office. She remembered something — she couldn't forget this either — something she'd never told another soul.

One summer morning a few years ago, arriving at the salon just after seven, Mrs. Brown had heard rumbling from Bonnie's office. Concerned, she'd rushed to her employer's aid that morning, too. She had discovered Bonnie akimbo upon her desk being made love to — the only polite term for the corpulent mashing that she saw — by Solomon Aquilino, owner of the barbershop next door.

Solomon, hairier than a goat, and Bonnie were married at the time, except not to each other.

Mrs. Brown might have been provincial, but she wasn't all that easy to shock. Seeing Bonnie and Solomon going at it had rattled her but did not shock her — well, so much corpulence in such fast motion was disturbing. It was an awful lot of flesh so early in the morning for her — for anyone — to see.

Bonnie had made her promise she would never say a word, and Mrs. Brown never did, not even telling Mrs. Fox when she asked that night how her day had gone. Her discretion endeared her to her boss, although Bonnie never made this apparent in the salon when the beauticians were around. Too bad, it would have helped Mrs. Brown. The beauticians were often dismissive and belittling.

"AAAAaaaaahhhhhmmmmm . . ."

Now, though, fearing the worst, Mrs. Brown rushed into Bonnie's office ready to grab the phone and call for an ambulance.

Bonnie, fully clothed in blue jeans, a blue and white striped, long-sleeve T-shirt, her platform pink espadrilles by her side, was seated on the floor in the lotus yoga position facing the full-length mirror on her office wall, and as she explained when she saw Mrs. Brown, she was chanting.

She waved her finely manicured right hand, her nails painted a deep black-red, and mouthed the words "skim latte doppio," her beverage of choice, which Mrs. Brown had learned how to make on the fancy espresso and cappuccino machine in the salon's kitchen. Besides cleaning and sweeping, her job included mending Bonnie's clothes and taking and making beverage orders for the staff and clientele. Sometimes, if the salon was very busy, she was given the okay to outsource the drinks order at the Village Cheese Shop next door, but her lattes, so carefully prepared, were better.

"My niece," Bonnie explained when Mrs. Brown returned with her coffee, "taught me last night how to chant for money — well, actually not money but for her guru's good grace and high, very high connections with the Source, which translates into abundance, which translates into money — and so that's what I was doing. I'm broke, well, like, I could be broke soon like every other motherfucker in this country. So I'm chanting. How are you?" Bonnie asked, ripping the corner of a packet of sugar substitute and pouring it into her latte.

Mrs. Brown's time at the beauty parlor rarely required that she divulge anything personal. No one inquired about her well-being, and that was okay; privacy is its own luxury. But today she offered some intimate detail of her own.

"Me, too. I am thinking about ways to find more money."

"Sssh, quiet," Bonnie said, her index finger to her lips. "My niece says to shore up our money potential we shouldn't talk about it with anyone. Never break the spell when you're incubating. I hope we already haven't said too much!"

The beauticians soon arrived, and the day was off full gallop, beginning with the first client, the wife of the mayor of Ashville, and she was dissatisfied with her color, again.

Mrs. Brown found the turquoise work jacket that she was required to wear (the beauticians could dress as they liked, which Mrs. Brown didn't mind because their choices in what they wore kept things interesting.) She grabbed her broom. Bonnie had given her a new one for Christmas along with a card that informed her that a donation in her name had been made to advance the efforts of the Dalai Lama. Mrs. Brown got to work, a full and busy day, a worker among workers, always a source of pride, except Mrs. Brown worked harder than anyone else at Bonnie's salon, so added to her pride was a fatigue she tried never to admit to.

CHAPTER 9

Probably all across America that night, in at least one out of every three households, someone was sitting at the kitchen table crunching numbers to see how and where they could find or make some extra, much-needed cash.

As Santo snoozed on bended paws at one end of the table, Mrs. Brown, pencil and pad in hand, sat at the other end reviewing her income and her expenses.

She had nothing in terms of art or furnishings she could sell. Concerning financial securities, there was a very modest investment in a retirement fund that she couldn't in all good conscience invade. In a savings-checking account was a slender stash of cash for April's taxes. To pay her monthly bills she relied not just on what she earned but also the income she received each month from Mrs. Fox, and now from Alice, who'd begun to contribute to the rent despite her grandmother's kind offer to pay it all herself.

No, she could not, she would not, ever think of raising her friend's rent. A few years ago, Mrs. Fox had proposed she might pay a bit more every month — not that she could afford any extra expense either. Mrs. Brown wouldn't hear of it.

"You're too good a friend, and too excellent a tenant," she said and immediately changed the subject.

What were her options? Her only reason to raise the rent now would be greed, and this, despite her dress calling to her, went against every spiritual principle she believed in.

She could try chanting, like Bonnie this morning. Except Mrs. Brown couldn't imagine herself chanting, making sounds like an old, cold seal on a slippery rock. She could advertise in the local newspaper for babysitting jobs in the evening, although parents weren't going out so much these nights because they too were saving their money. Ashville's restaurants were suffering as a result. There were lottery tickets, of course. Mrs. Brown, unlike everyone she knew, never bought these. She considered them an obsession and a waste of time — hoping, watching for the results, being disappointed when one didn't score; they were little paper heartbreakers.

Maybe it was time to reconsider? Just the other day, the television news had been filled with the good-luck story of a twenty-three-year-old, dirt-poor rancher in South Dakota who won $232.1 million in the Powerball lottery.

"I want to thank the Lord for giving me this opportunity and blessing me with this great fortune. I will not squander it," the rancher said as he took a lump-sum payout of $118 million.

Mrs. Brown was looking in her kitchen cupboards for signs of any purchases she could do without in the future when Alice tapped at her door.

Seeing the cupboards opened, the yellow legal pad on the table with an itemized list, her open checkbook . . . Alice figured that Mrs. Brown had been laid off today.

"Everything okay?" Alice asked with great concern.

Mrs. Brown paused. "Sure it is. No complaints. In fact, I never had it so good."

The women laughed. Mrs. Brown explained to Alice that was something a beloved uncle used to answer, regardless of the real truth, when you asked him how he was. "Always tell a better story, Emilia," he would say. "And you'll feel better." He was the same uncle who also always insisted she take second helpings when she ate at his house. "Eat, Emilia, eat. We'll say you ate anyway."

Mrs. Brown was so prepared to pinch pennies that tonight she thought twice before putting the kettle on for tea, since doing so involved the cost of electricity.

Alice watched the older woman; she seemed a bit jumbled up somehow. Something about Mrs. Brown's expression told Alice more than tea was in order tonight.

"I have been having trouble sleeping the past few nights," she lied to help Mrs. Brown say yes, "and I was wondering if you might want to have a glass of my grandmother's sherry with me. It will make me sleepy, but I wouldn't drink alone."

That wasn't entirely true. Alice was very happy to drink alone, a bottle of wine, a bath filled with bubbles, and maybe a joint? Add some great music, and it was a recipe for bliss.

One of Mrs. Fox's best customers at the bookshop had given Mrs. Fox a bottle of dry sherry every year for Christmas. She uncorked the bottle only on New Year's Eve so she and Mrs. Brown could toast the new year, and pretty much the rest of the year it stayed on a kitchen shelf. There were six bottles left.

"But it is only Thursday night," Mrs. Brown said. Saturday seemed the only acceptable night to have a drink. Drinking on weeknights was decadent or, worse, a sign there was a problem. Mr. Brown had drunk on weeknights. Not in the beginning, when they were first married, but later, toward middle age, every night drinks and eventually every night drunk.

Still, getting out of her kitchen meant getting away from thinking about the past, at least for right now. Having something as relaxing as a bit of Mrs. Fox's sherry did appeal to her. Mrs. Brown followed Alice to her living room across the way. Alice poured the sherry in short-stemmed crystal glasses that had originally belonged to her great-grandmother. She poured the sherry almost to the top of the glass. Again, Mrs. Brown thought, It's the difference in our generations. We'd never pour that high.

Two sips of sherry and Mrs. Brown told all. About what had happened when she saw Mrs. Groton's suit dress, and about the novel Rachel Ames had given her, *Mrs. 'Arris Goes to Paris,* which could be a blueprint for how she might get her dress.

"That's a lot of money you will need to save, Mrs. Brown," Alice said. "In the novel, which I'd like to borrow if that's okay with you, how does Mrs. Harris save for hers?"

"I haven't finished reading it. I am not the fast reader that you are or your grandmother is," Mrs. Brown said. "But as far as I got last night she was doing without extras, like the bunch of flowers she'd buy herself on the weekend. Then she wins a football pool. She wins big, I guess."

"That easy, really? Then what happens?"

"That's as far as I read. In fact," Mrs. Brown said, "that's as far as I'm going to read."

"Why?" Alice asked.

"Because, Alice, if it doesn't have a happy ending, I do not want to know."

Lest Mrs. Brown feel anything less than enthusiasm and support, Alice resisted the urge to ask too many more questions. But she explained that if this was really and truly something she wanted to do, then once Mrs. Brown had saved up the money, she wouldn't have to go to New York to buy the dress. She could shop online, like most people Alice's age do. Even people Alice's mother's age, late forties, shop online. Everyone does.

Mrs. Brown smiled but didn't respond, nor would she tonight. That Alice didn't understand was clear to her. Why the sudden urgency for the odyssey ahead? Mrs. Brown had only a slightly better understanding. She couldn't articulate more, not yet.

It was getting late. Mrs. Brown thanked her young friend for the tipple of sherry. It certainly had worked its soothing charms. Before she returned to her place, she reminded Alice that she'd mentioned something about a tweed jacket she'd gotten from the Ashville Thrift Shop that didn't fit quite right? Mrs. Brown had an idea for fixing the problem that she'd like to try.

"Tomorrow night, we'll have a look," Mrs. Brown said. "I'm no Oscar de la Renta, but probably there's a seam or two I can do something with." She added, "No charge, I mean. Just so you know that, after all this talk about money."

Alice walked Mrs. Brown to the door. "You know, Mrs. Brown, about going to New York, I'll come with you if you want. I know the city okay enough. I did an internship there three summers ago. Remember? That's when I visited Granny here in Ashville before I went back home in August."

While she carefully washed and dried her grandmother's sherry glasses, Alice reflected on Mrs. Brown's resolution to save for a suit like Mrs. Groton's and then go all the way to New York to buy it.

It was weird, and it didn't make any sense to her.

Looking at the time, a bit before 11:00 P.M., she figured that, given the time difference, her grandmother would be cleaning up after dinner in Vancouver and sitting down to read whatever book it was she was reading this week.

Alice telephoned, and Mrs. Fox answered on the first ring.

"What's wrong, Alice? It's late for you with teaching early tomorrow morning."

When it came to understanding Mrs. Brown, and keeping her word to her grandmother to support her, Alice was out of her element on this "go-to-New-York-and-buy-a-dress thing," as she called it — and would call it again many times over.

"I mean what, Granny, like, what the fuck, right? It's only a black jacket and dress. It's an effing suit. What's that? So boring!"

"Don't swear, Alice, it isn't ladylike and much more is expected of a college-educated person," Mrs. Fox said. "Use words that reflect your intelligence, not your slang."

This was exasperating, but Alice pressed on. "Yes, Granny, sorry. Big words. Coming right up. As polysyllabic as possible."

Mrs. Fox laughed. She was slow if ever to admit it, but she enjoyed her youngest granddaughter's punkish attitudes — sometimes.

"What don't you understand about a woman of a certain age wanting to step out of her shell and travel somewhere, in this case New York, where she has never been, and to buy a dress?" Mrs. Fox asked. "Just because it might be found online? And I would have thought you'd like this suit that Emilia is wanting. It's black, after all, your favorite color."

"Well, yes, there's that. It's black, that's a plus, but don't they sell boring black dresses at Penny's?" Alice took a breath, and continued. "It's a suit, Granny, it is utilitarian. It isn't fantastic, it won't be pretty and it will be dull. No matter how well made it is. If she's going for something so expensive, there are lots of other dresses, beautiful dresses, red carpet dresses. She's missing the opportunity to have something that makes her feel young and sexy, or is that the idea? Maybe she can get something that's great and gets her more attention, you know, from men — she isn't too old for men, is she; people your age still do it, don't they, Granny? But with this suit, I don't get it, she'll look like a lawyer. And she isn't a lawyer. She's just a cleaning lady in a beauty shop."

Mrs. Fox waited to respond. It's always best to let the young empty the tank when they are ranting. "I want to tell you something about women like Mrs. Brown, and like myself, really, living on small fixed incomes, we'd give anything to be accepted in a boardroom, if the fashion world only understood that. We don't all want to be sexpots, or cougars, or just covered up in droopy blouses and trousers. There's also something alluring, very, very alluring about a dress that is perfectly correct. But in an effort to make my generation disappear, no one sells clothing that empowers us. There's only ridicule, condescension, or dismissal."

Alice had never thought about it this way. Could a really well-made suit dress be as much a fantasy for a woman as an evening gown or, in Alice's case, one of the amazing leather jackets that designers like Rick Owens or Ann Demeuelemeester make but that only heiresses and rock stars can afford?

"Sometimes a dress is not just a dress," Mrs. Fox said. "It's a symbol."

"I get it, Granny," Alice said. "Sometimes a cigar is just a cigar, and sometimes it's a penis, a big swinging symbol, that's what

98

you mean."

"Alice!"

"Oh, come on, Granny. Lighten up."

Mrs. Fox would. Lighten up, that is, as she continued to explain to Alice that Mrs. Brown obviously felt she needed this bold plan, this late-in-life odyssey, and for reasons that were none of their business unless Mrs. Brown disclosed them herself.

"We won't press her to discuss it and we won't analyze it," Mrs. Fox told Alice. "And it's probably much more respectful not to ask when she planned on wearing it once she gets it, assuming of course that she can and does get it. How *is* she going to manage that, I wonder."

More would be revealed, and their job as friends was to just get out of the way, wait patiently for more details, and be supportive throughout.

"Keep me posted about this, please, Alice?" Mrs. Fox said before they hung up. "I love you and I love how you're taking an interest in others, especially someone like Emilia. I do realize that she is so different than you or anyone you know."

After the call, Mrs. Fox, subdued and concerned, looked out the kitchen window of her place in Vancouver to where a strong oak stood. How well it still looked, and probably would in spring, too, no matter what hell of weather this winter brought.

Trees survive winter and are revived by spring — so much hope in the cycle of nature — but people? People weather away unless spring keeps in their hearts.

Mrs. Fox was glad for the news about Mrs. Brown. Even if it was just a dress and jacket, it was a beginning. How people endure the complexities of their lives with faith and cheer, finding their own measure of hope, is one of the constant miracles, and often surprises, of life.

But her friend's first trip to New York would be a daunting prospect, just as saving enough money to buy the dress would be.

Mrs. Fox would do everything to support Mrs. Brown and wished she could be there in person to do so. Instead, she vowed to make sure that her granddaughter, Alice, did a great job in her place. But there was just one more thing . . . was it too late to call home to Rhode Island?

Mrs. Fox dialed. Alice, who was checking her various social media accounts as she always did last thing before lights-out, answered on the third ring.

Alice was scrolling through Instagram, her favorite new hashtag — #MarieAntoi-netteInBellBottoms — postings of recognizable fashion and other celebrity people wearing outrageously priced bohemian styles.

"Granny, what's wrong?"

"Nothing's wrong. Just something I wanted to say about Mrs. Brown."

"Yes, Granny?"

"That book Mrs. Brown read? What was it called? The one you said she wasn't going to finish reading because she didn't want to know how it ends?"

Alice couldn't remember the title, but she remembered the book.

"I've read everything, but I don't recall this book," Mrs. Fox said. "I want you to read it. Will you, Alice? See how it ends."

Alice promised her grandmother that she would.

CHAPTER 10

It was interesting, so Mrs. Brown thought, that the topic at the beauty parlor the next morning was money, as it probably was in shops and offices all over the world.

Mrs. Brown had opened up shop, donned her turquoise work jacket, grabbed a broom, and started sweeping when Bonnie blew into the shop in a state of apoplexy.

"Coffee?" She could barely get the word out.

When Bonnie wanted coffee, rather than her usual latte, Mrs. Brown knew that something was troubling her employer, that she would have been up late worrying, or not slept at all, smoking something "herbal," as she would occasionally admit, and drinking red wine.

Mrs. Brown brought the coffee, black with two sugar substitutes, in Bonnie's favorite mug. The words "Love Spoken Here" were written in script on it.

Slumped in the chair by the cash register, Bonnie sipped the coffee. (When revived, she would perch herself on a swivel stool right at the cash register.) "Business is slow, Mrs. Brown, I don't know if you've noticed? I mean, people are still coming in for the hair, but they aren't booking the other services, manicures and pedicures, and facials, which means they aren't buying any of the skin products. I might have to let one of the beauticians go."

Mrs. Brown lowered her head, and did not know what to say. She instinctively knew if anyone was let go it would be Teresa, the youngest of the six beauticians that Bonnie employed, also the nicest, if not the brightest.

"I don't know what Teresa will do if I let her go," Bonnie said, confirming Mrs. Brown's fears. "Her husband is a son of a bitch — oh, sorry, Mrs. Brown, excuse the French — and she is supporting him. In fact, she has taken the morning off to go with him to a job interview. But I have to watch every penny. It's this economy. It is not a time for carelessness with your money. I hope you've saved a lot over the years; you should have. I don't see you have many extravagances, must be one of the advantages of getting old, isn't it? You crave less."

Mrs. Brown thought about her perfect black suit dress and resumed sweeping and tidying up. Bonnie kept talking. "I can't stand to listen to the news anymore, all the gloom and doom about the economy." She closed the cash register and crossed the room to the window onto Main Street, looking south as if she was expecting someone. "I started screaming at the NBC news last night, 'Tell a better story, asshole! Tell a better story!' "

She turned away from the window and smiled. "But the anchorman didn't," Bonnie said.

The beauty parlor opened for business. The beauticians positioned themselves at their chairs waiting for the first customers of the day. The place began to buzz. Moments after her first client had left her chair, one of the senior beauticians, Hillie, a sassy brunette from South Carolina who relocated with her first husband to Rhode Island several years ago, rushed up to Bonnie at the register.

"Old Mrs. Casey just told me she couldn't afford to give me a tip!" Hillie exclaimed.

"Why not?" Bonnie asked.

Hillie leaned in and whispered as if she was telling some kind of dirty secret. "Says she is cutting back. Has to. Reduce expenses. Well, get her. Isn't she one of the richest dames in Ashville?"

Bonnie nodded. "Maybe the richest, now that Millicent Groton has gone to the big charity ball in the sky."

Georgie, a curvaceous beautician in her mid-forties with a salad of curls on her head the color of ripe red plums, overheard this exchange and joined in. "I didn't want to say anything, but two of my customers have asked me for a discount."

Bonnie gasped. "What did you tell them?"

"I told them, Discuss it with Bonnie, she's the boss," Georgie answered, pouring herself a cup of coffee.

"Discounts!" Bonnie exclaimed. "What the fuck do they think this is, the Red Cross? Free blowouts and free facials!"

As the morning wound down toward noon, there was one last customer left before business picked up again during lunchtime (followed by a lull in the afternoon, and then again a hectic period after five until closing at seven). The customer was Mary Smithers, owner of the local shoe shop, and a kindred spirit with the beauticians because they were all Main Street businesswomen — as opposed to the local grandees, the well-heeled married or single ladies. Their conversation concerned the current economy.

"The one good thing about the bad economy I am glad for is that 'bling' is over. Not in good taste anymore now that austerity is fashionable. I won't have to sell so many god-awful gaudy shoes, like those gladiator sandals last season with coins dangling all over, so damn ugly," Mary said, digging in her brown suede handbag for a Life Saver. She had been trying to quit smoking, and the Life Savers, butterscotch, were meant to help. Three years later she was still smoking, and eating three rolls of butterscotch a day.

The women, except Mrs. Brown, gathered around the cash register. Bonnie perched on her swivel stool, the queen bee. Mrs. Brown cleaned and dusted on the sidelines, and listened.

"Why do you want 'bling' to be over? It was pretty. It was sexy. It was hot, honey. And I just hate dull," said Francie Brunie, another beautician. "Dull gives me hives."

"Hives aren't dull," Mary said, and laughed. "They itch."

Francie pressed on. "Any of you looked at the new clothes in the fashion magazines lately? They're either freakish, perfect for stoned Amish people, boiled wool and the like, or they are simply dull, not dressy, you know, for old ladies."

Francie was preening in the mirror on the wall behind Bonnie, arranging her lemon-yellow helmet of hair and applying a new pink lipstick. "Who wants to look like old Mrs. Brown here?" she said, not trying too hard to whisper. "Have you ever seen such a dull thing in your life? I mean, I feel sorry for her, you know, I really do, but still, come on, honey, put on some lipstick, will you? Add some color! Boost your aura."

Over by the sinks, where she was cleaning up after the beauticians, Mrs. Brown pretended not to have heard what Francie said and not to have noticed that no one disagreed. Always polite, she retreated into the good manners of turning the other cheek, "rising above," and remaining kind. Here Mrs. Brown was brave. In today's frightened world, kindness takes courage sometimes.

She just kept on. She wiped hair cuttings off chairs and swept under the shelves and sinks. This wasn't the first time something like this had happened, and it would not be the last time either. Mrs. Brown told herself she was here to work, not here running for Miss Popularity. Besides, she had other things to think about. Her plan for getting her dress!

"Well, everyone I know is trying to make

107

some extra dough, me included," said Hillie. "I'm starting to charge for it."

"Charge for what?" Mary asked.

Hillie laughed and patted her ample buttocks dressed in paisley stretch corduroy pants worn with high, black heels.

The other women giggled.

"Laugh all you want, girls," Bonnie said, "but this is really serious. The economy is tricky business, especially for us women. I find nothing funny about it."

Hillie shook her head. "Honey, why do people say not to be funny? It seems to me that is the least you can do these days. Make a joke." She paused and lowered her voice. "At least *we* have careers," she said, looking in Mrs. Brown's direction but avoiding catching her eye. "I feel sorry for the women who get by willy-nilly. If things get any worse, they are the ones who are going to suffer the most."

Everyone at Bonnie's thought they knew everything there was to know about Mrs. Brown's life, but they didn't. You only really come close to knowing another person when you can begin to identify with their feelings. They were clueless about Mrs. Brown.

The earliest of the lunchtime customers began arriving for their haircuts, colorings, and coifs. The click-clack midday conversation sounded like a concert of so many spoons on jelly glasses. Teresa came in, apologizing to anyone who would listen for taking the morning off. But she hoped her husband's job interview went well. He needed moral support.

Bonnie, still enthroned at the cash register, was reading the *Ashville Bulletin* and offering her commentary on the local news. She supported the farmers' market trying to get more space on Mystic Green near the river on summer Saturdays; she was against the fire station selling air rights so Verizon could put up a cellular phone tower. (The phone company was offering $35,000.) When she got to the television listings and saw that Suze Orman, the money guru, was going to be a guest on one of the afternoon chat shows today, talking about "how to make the bad economy good for you," she exclaimed her delight.

"It's a sign from God! From the Goddess!" Bonnie said.

She decided to feign a headache after lunch and go home early to watch the show, after which she would chant for prosperity and abundance for an hour before Solomon Aquilino stopped in. (She'd buy wine — California chardonnay could be bought cheap — on the way home.) She asked Mrs.

Brown to lock up after all the beauticians finished their work.

Of course Mrs. Brown obliged.

Bonnie was off. Zipping herself into her black motorcycle-style shearling jacket, she smiled in the direction of the cleanup woman. How Bonnie envied Mrs. Brown. She lived such a simple life. Without any great expectations, she had no disappointments a cup of hot tea and a night in front of the television — watching nature programs, no doubt — couldn't cure.

CHAPTER 11

Alice had also read the television listings and as a result tuned in to the afternoon chat show with Suze Orman. She even took notes. Not just because it would make her grandmother happy that she was looking out for her friend and neighbor, but because Alice had decided she wanted to do whatever she could to help Mrs. Brown.

It had been on her mind all day.

She hadn't yet connected the dots back to Mrs. Brown and her desire to help, but Alice had been asked to help organize a parent-teacher conference in January called the Village Effect. This was also the name of a recently published book that discussed how the loss of human contact in the Internet age was not just, according to research studies, literally shortening adult lives but turning children into robots — uncaring, unfeeling, isolated robots. One study even found that in dual-income, two- or three-child families, a third of the family members were never in the same room at the same time.

Even Alice, who in her teen years had liked nothing better than the absence of her immediate relations in any room of the house at any given time, was alarmed by this statistic and what it portended for her students' development.

These months in bucolic, small-town Ashville, living in her grandmother's quiet home, becoming friendly with the older woman across the hall, had changed Alice's thinking about certain things. One of these things was that it takes a village — not only to raise children, as the expression says — but also to feel contented.

It was nice to feel like a part of a community, a neighbor amongst neighbors.

Keeping separate, feeling superior — something she had always prided herself on — wasn't the enlivener she'd thought it was when she was a stoner teen and college student.

Having her first real job was a real eye-opener. Trudging to work on time day after day — no later than 7:00 A.M. — she realized that there is great nobility in routine and also great sacrifice. Getting out of bed took tremendous effort for Alice still, and a lot of self-talk, caffeine, and blasting music. Some days her personal best was just getting to the job on time.

As she got to know her colleagues, especially the much older ones, who'd been working for decades, she saw that it's not easy day after day after day to show up to a job whether you feel like it or not, put in decent effort, earn a meager wage — keep cool and polite when things don't go your way, your students don't respect you, or some boss angers or bullies you — then go home and basically spend the few remaining hours of your day getting ready for tomorrow.

Thanks to the examples of her colleagues, and to Mrs. Brown as well, Alice was realizing how lucky she was to still be young, energized by her hopes and her dreams, even her hormones: getting some teaching experience under her belt in Ashville, then moving to a big city, maybe San Francisco or New York, a better job, a cool guy, maybe marry him, but certainly live with him; travel with him to places that interested her, like Berlin and Japan; maybe have a kid, maybe even two; get a vacation house near the water, like that. Have sex all the time . . .

Mrs. Brown, on the other hand, had come around and around on this wearying wheel many times already. How that must feel? When every excitement you ever hoped for or imagined had happened or it hadn't, and now you knew it never would. What was left? What was there to look forward to? Too much old age and not enough money, and memories that, in Mrs. Brown's case, weren't all of them happy.

"A secret grief," her grandmother had said when she and Alice spoke most recently on the telephone. "She's a simple, rural woman with a secret grief, try and remember that. God will bless you, Alice, if you just try and see life through her eyes, not your own," Mrs. Fox said.

The concept of seeing life from someone else's perspective was kind of revolutionary, too, and it was something anyone with even the tiniest capacity for imagination could do, but do enough of us try? Alice wondered.

Close your eyes and catch a glimpse of her neighbor's life through her eyes, and what did you see? Alice saw what she always saw when she pictured Mrs. Brown: head bowed, standing in her kitchen, her hands on the countertop as if it was the back of the pew in front of you in church, or the railing of a ship lost at sea.

When the theory of empathy becomes a

rhythm of the heart, it's a big deal in a young person's life. So why not watch and see what this money guru had to say? It might help Mrs. Brown, and it might also benefit Alice. Lord knows, she could use a few money-saving tips.

Alice watched Suze Orman while dinner was baking in the oven. A tuna casserole from an ancient recipe that was her grandmother's favorite standby — the recipe was scribbled on an index card stuck in a copy of the Ashville telephone book.

Alice needed to practice her cooking skills.

She had a second date on Saturday with Milo, Milo Benjamin was his full name, and she had invited him home for dinner. Milo was a guy Alice had met on Tinder, a dating website that was more trouble than it was worth when she was in a big place like Vancouver — separating the wheat, so to speak, from the chaff — but was proving useful in this part of the world, where there weren't many occasions, or places, where young people could hang out if they weren't students on the Guilford campus.

There was the tavern on Main Street, but it was mostly older men, or rowdy younger guys from the town; some were hot, for sure. But although always up for the pleasures of the flesh, Alice had enough self-respect not to be blindly promiscuous, and she didn't trust that Ashville guys would get her. The way she dressed, all in black, a city girl.

Alice also knew that a schoolteacher, especially a young single teacher living in a new town, should always consider the impression she gave people, particularly the parents of her students. This was something her school's principal had talked about during teacher orientation in late August, mentioning the tavern as a place to avoid, for the women teachers as well as the men.

Maybe it was too soon to invite Milo for a home-cooked meal, but she'd risk it.

A few years older than Alice, Milo was an English teacher at a boarding school in northeastern Connecticut, about a sixty-minute drive from Ashville. For their first date, two weeks ago, they had met equal distance in Woodstock, Connecticut.

Conversation was easy once Alice stopped judging Milo's conservative clothing — a sandy-brown corduroy sport jacket, a white polo shirt, and khakis. (And when Milo stopped sizing up Alice, no longer daunted by the I'LL STOP WEARING BLACK WHEN THEY INVENT A DARKER COLOR T-shirt, the tight black jeans — which he liked, they were naughty — motorcycle boots, black chiffon scarf, and thick peacock-blue eye-liner. Besides, she'd arrived in a 2003 gray Ford Focus — "my grandmother's car," she said — so how dangerous could she be?)

Milo had mentioned during this first date that he liked visiting Ashville whenever he had the chance because the town's greens were "perfectly articulated." What could Alice say in response except to invite him to visit?

"Why don't you come to dinner?"

"I'd love that," Milo said without hesitation. "When?"

The tuna casserole recipe was easy enough and, she hoped, foolproof: a can of Campbell's mushroom soup, a can of tuna, three cups of cooked extrawide egg noodles, three-quarters of a cup of milk, a favorite regional brand of potato chips called State Line hand-crunched for the casserole crust, top and bottom, and all baked for twenty-five minutes at 400 degrees.

As soon as Alice heard Mrs. Brown return home, she telephoned her.

"I've been cooking," she told her neighbor.

"Are you okay?" Mrs. Brown answered.

Alice laughed. She explained that she had a date tomorrow night with this interesting man named Milo, who was driving almost an hour to taste her cooking, and that she

117

wanted to try the casserole out on Mrs. Brown before she made it for Milo.

Mrs. Brown appreciated the offer of a hot meal after a long day and invited Alice and her casserole to her kitchen table (so Alice wouldn't have to do dishes. They'd share the effort of the meal). She told Alice to bring the tweed jacket she wanted altered with her; Mrs. Brown put the kettle on for tea. She liked hot tea with her meals.

After they'd exchanged formalities and pleasantries, the tuna casserole was dished out in generous but not overly large servings on white china plates and the teapot positioned in the middle of the table, Mrs. Brown reached for her handbag — it was next to her feet — and opened it.

"Look," she said, producing three lottery tickets for the weekend's big win.

"I thought you disapproved of the lottery," Alice said, pouring the tea. "Remember when I bought a bunch of tickets when I first got here from Vancouver?"

"I do remember. Something about beginner's luck, you said, now that you were living in a new place." Mrs. Brown tasted the tuna casserole. "It's good, Alice. Congratulations."

It was fine, the casserole was just fine; Mrs. Brown suggested Alice serve it to Milo with a side of peas and a green salad. Or include the peas in the casserole. Beige food needed something green for color with it, especially if you were serving it to a date.

"Really, peas?" Alice wondered. "Don't you think peas are old? I mean, old-fashioned? I was thinking arugula or kale. Kale is very happening right now."

"Oh, is it? Kale is very happening?" Mrs. Brown said, and laughed.

She's stuck on peas, Alice thought, and wouldn't push the kale on her. Alice returned to the topic of the lottery tickets. "So what's this about buying lottery tickets?"

"Well, I have been thinking about how to pay for my dress and the trip to New York City, and since it is such an exceptional thing to want," Mrs. Brown said, rising from the table to refill Santo's water bowl, "I just thought it might call for an exceptional method of getting the money. So I bought the tickets."

Alice smiled. "Wouldn't it be something if you won, Mrs. Brown, and you became a millionaire? Isn't the pot worth something like $265 million?"

"I shouldn't have bought any tickets, really," Mrs. Brown said with a deep sigh, and returned to the table with Santo following. She put the lottery tickets back in her pocketbook and snapped the clasp closed. "Or I should have only bought one."

Alice didn't understand. "Why just one?"

"Well, I think if God wants me to win the lottery, then one ticket would be enough, wouldn't it?"

"But haven't you maximized your chances by buying three? You know, helped God out kind of thing."

Mrs. Brown shook her head. "If God wants me to win the lottery, then one ticket would be enough. Buying more than one shows him that I lack faith, and without faith, Alice, no one is going to win anything except disappointment."

Alice wasn't raised with much religion, and this sort of talk made her uncomfortable. All she knew was that something that seemed to appear on Instagram at least once a month sounded right: "Religion is for people who are afraid of going to hell; spirituality is for people who have been to hell."

Alice rested her fork on her plate. "When it comes to the topic of God and money, I figure it's like what they say in gambling terms, a crabshoot."

"Crapshoot," Mrs. Brown said, correcting Alice. "I think the gambling term is 'crapshoot,' not 'crabshoot.' "

Alice shrugged. "Crab is much more colorful, don't you think? And probably much easier to shoot than" — she leaned in and whispered — "than crap."

"Alice!" Mrs. Brown responded. She wasn't really shocked, but as the elder adult in the room felt obliged to register some distress.

"Well, I doubt very much that God is thinking much about my dress. Maybe I am being impractical. And, you know," Mrs. Brown said, "standing in that line at the store to buy these tickets? Everyone looked so dazed, and so needy, so possessed by fantasies about money and their expectations. Me, too, I suppose."

Mrs. Brown stood up and began to clear the table. Alice got up, too, and offered to help, but Mrs. Brown declined and told her to sit. Alice lifted Santo to her lap, and the cat purred his delight.

"So I watched Suze Orman on Granny's television this afternoon," Alice said, "and I jotted down some notes that I hope help you save up the money you need."

Mrs. Brown returned to the table with a blue tin of store-bought Scandinavian butter cookies. Note to self: no more store-bought Scandinavian butter cookies. Cut costs.

"This Suze Orman is intense, isn't she?" Alice said, turning the pages of the yellow legal pad where she'd scribbled her notes. "And so blond. That's a TV thing, I think. On TV, the older they get, the blonder they get."

Santo was now in Mrs. Brown's lap.

Alice read aloud: " 'Hope for the best, plan for the worst.' 'Financial responsibility comes from active responsibility.' I wasn't entirely sure what that meant. 'If you plan for life's what-ifs, there's no need to panic.' 'Wishful thinking can lead to financial ruin.' 'If you can't afford it today, it's just going to be worse tomorrow.' "

Alice stopped reading. "That's not a lot of positive thinking, is it?"

Mrs. Brown didn't answer.

"But it is practical advice," Alice said. "Suze is so enthusiastic about the positive outcome from it, so . . ."

Santo jumped on top of the kitchen table. Mrs. Brown lifted him to the floor. Looking inside her pocketbook, she found a scrap of paper, an envelope from the beauty shop.

"I've been working on a list of things to cut back to save money," Mrs. Brown said, reaching for a pair of drugstore reading glasses she kept in the fruit bowl on the kitchen table. Old and scratched, they sloped on her nose like Christmas tinsel tossed on a thin bough.

She read her list: "Cancel delivery of *Ashville Bulletin.* No dry cleaning. No new summer shoes. No more store-bought cookies," she said, staring at the tin of butter cookies. "No movies . . ."

"No movies?" Alice exclaimed.

Despite the fact that there were very few films they ever felt the need to see, Alice knew that Mrs. Brown and her grandmother enjoyed their occasional nights at the movies. And if she and Mrs. Brown ever agreed on wanting to see the same film, she'd be happy to take her.

"No movies," Mrs. Brown said, continuing to read her list. "Generic products instead of name brands, including," she whispered, looking in Santo's direction, "cat food. Winter will cost me, but you know if you use a hot water bottle to warm the bed, you can keep your heating bills down. What else? Cancel cable television . . ."

Alice, about to reach for a third cookie, didn't out of respect for the new austerity plan. "But if you don't have a computer, you need to have television, don't you? What if there is a national emergency?"

"Bad news travels fast enough," Mrs. Brown answered. "I am sure, God forbid there's a national emergency, that the news will find me."

"Well, you can watch Granny's TV, anytime you like. I'm mostly watching things on my computer," Alice said, and paused. "Since I'm subletting, maybe you want to add something to my rent . . ."

Mrs. Brown answered: "Never that."

"Then I hope you'll let me treat you to the movies sometime?" Alice asked. "And let me pay you for the work you do on my jacket?"

Mrs. Brown wasn't going to let Alice pay for the movies. "Didn't I tell you, no charge for the alterations. But please try the jacket on. Let me see what I can do."

Alice stood and did as told. Santo jumped up and took her place on the chair she'd just occupied. Mrs. Brown pinched and pulled at the jacket and sure enough found a couple of seams she could work with. As she did, she told Alice some of her ideas for earning extra income, in addition to the ideas for saving on expenses she'd already mentioned.

During her break tomorrow Mrs. Brown would stop at the dry cleaners on Main Street, and also at the men's clothing shop, to offer her sewing services in case they needed any extra help. The hospital might need someone in the kitchen on Sundays. She'd suggest to Bonnie that she inventory her stockroom, where all the beauty supplies were kept; that could be a few extra dollars if she worked a few nights after the salon closed.

Just having these ideas made her feel optimistic. "Where there's a will, there's a way, isn't there, Alice?" Mrs. Brown asked.

Alice sounded absolutely and perfectly convincing when she answered, "Yes, Mrs. Brown, you're right!"

Later that night, when Alice was getting ready for bed, and even past lights-out, her evening's visit with Mrs. Brown remained very much on her mind.

I may not always understand Mrs. Brown, I mean, *really* not understand her, but I guess that's okay? I guess that's just Mrs. Brown, she thought.

Alice smiled. And she's *my* Mrs. Brown.

A quiet sense of happiness came to Alice then. Tonight she had belonged somewhere, even as unlikely as it was given the difference in their ages and lifestyles. She'd been helpful, and kind, and the courtesy, and concern, had been reciprocated. Was there any need, any pressing need, to wonder why or how or what it meant?

Alice didn't think so. Not tonight. Acceptance and understanding were plenty explanation enough, at least for now.

CHAPTER 12

Fear is criminal. IT steals from life. In the planning and plotting for her perfect dress, Mrs. Brown remembered a story she'd heard told in church many, many years ago.

The pastor, who was given to referencing the early-twentieth-century spiritual leader Emmet Fox, no relation to her friend and neighbor Sarah Fox that she was aware of, was preaching that one needed to realize that fear is a bluffer. "Call its bluff, and it collapses," he exclaimed, and continued quoting Fox verbatim.

He described an amusing incident that allegedly took place at a town in the countryside in Holland. A lion escaped from a traveling circus. Not far away a housewife was sewing near the open window of her living room. The animal suddenly sprang in, dashed by her like a flash, rushed into the hall, and took refuge in the triangular cupboard under the staircase. The startled woman supposed it to be a donkey and, indignant at the muddy prints it left on her clean floor, pursued it into the dark closet among the brooms and pans, and proceeded to thrash it unmercifully with a broom. The animal shook with terror, and the angry woman redoubled the force of her blows. Then four men arrived with guns and nets and recaptured the animal. The terrified lion gave himself up quietly, only too glad to escape that woman torturing him.

When the woman discovered that she had been beating a lion, she fainted dead away.

She had dominion over him for as long as she thought he was a donkey, and as long as she treated him as a donkey, the lion was in abject fear of her. When she discovered her mistake, the old preconditioned fear returned and she responded according to the fear, not her faith.

This anecdote proved a galvanizing recollection for Mrs. Brown. She needed its encouragement because nearly four months and one long cold winter since declaring her intention to turn lions into donkeys, her ideas for earning extra money were pretty much a bust.

She made $132 taking in some sewing from the dry cleaners. Yes, she broke her rule about not buying lottery tickets, not once, but twice, and lost her money.

Meanwhile, every day was business as usual at Bonnie's beauty parlor, well, that is until it wasn't. On a Tuesday afternoon in late March something, or someone, you might say, rather extraordinary happened.

Just before five, the door to the salon opened and alighting in the entrance was a woman who took all by total surprise. Except when they'd visited Mrs. Groton back in the day, celebrities were unusual in Ashville.

Even Mrs. Brown knew who this was. When she was cleaning and a cover of one of the celebrity magazines Bonnie subscribed to caught her eye, she'd have a look.

Sailing through the doorway of the salon, long, tawny brownish hair flicking over her shoulders as if airborne in a sultry Caribbean breeze, her skin as luscious as French chestnuts . . .

What was the supermodel Florida Noble doing in Ashville? Really? At Bonnie's Beauty Salon?

It took a lot to bring Bonnie's to a full stop, but this did it. Florida Noble wore impossibly tight but chic, not vulgar, white jeans — legs as long as highways, waist smaller than a shot glass. Below them she wore sandy khaki-colored strappy sandals with a five-inch stiletto heel. Above them she wore a paper-thin black cashmere T-shirt and a brown suede blazer. Florida Noble, supermodel — Dolce & Gabbana, Virgin Atlantic airlines, Louis Vuitton — magnificent mare, was in need of some beauty assistance.

Bonnie's sandpaper voice — she was chanting to excess morning, noon, and night for money, and the herbal cigarettes weren't helping — trembled.

"What are you doing here? I mean, oh, that's rude. Hello. *Hello!* Come in. Come in. I'm Bonnie. This is my salon. What brings you to Ashville, Miss Noble? May I offer you some coffee? Tea? Water?"

Florida shook Bonnie's hand. "Call me Florida, please. And, yes, do you have coffee? Oh, I would just absolutely love some. I was looking for a Starbucks but couldn't find one this morning. I guess there isn't Starbucks in Ashville? How extraordinary, the only part of the world I have ever been to without a Starbucks!" she said, her cadence a cultured singsong.

She rested her extra-large, navy blue Hermès Birkin bag on the counter near Bonnie's cash register.

Florida was embarrassed when Bonnie shooed Mrs. Brown into the kitchen to get the coffee. Mrs. Brown returned with the hot beverage in a white mug, a small pitcher of cream, and a sugar bowl on a faux-silver tray.

Florida took the mug. Something about the decency of this scrawny but gracious woman had instantly touched her heart.

"I'm Florida," she said, extending her hand.

Mrs. Brown bowed her head slightly.

"And you are?"

"Emilia Brown," Mrs. Brown said, taking Florida's hand.

"Now, now, Mrs. Brown, you mustn't monopolize our esteemed guest," Bonnie said. And to Florida: "You must be lost?"

Mrs. Brown retreated with her tray to the kitchen and returned with her broom.

Florida explained what had brought her to Ashville. "I am in what is the equivalent of my senior year at Guilford," she said, referring to the college just on the outskirts of town. "I've been able to do the entire four years in three by studying during the summers and corresponding with my professors, but I'm required to spend the better part of my last semester on campus for my final exams and orals. So . . . ."

She opened her pocketbook and rummaged through it. "I just arrived yesterday in New York from Paris, where I was shooting, and just got up here to Ashville today and have to get back to New York tonight and shoot in the morning and then come back to Ashville Sunday night in time for a meeting with my adviser Monday morning and by the following Monday I have to be in residence here" — she spoke as fast as some photographers shoot film — "but I am going to commute to and from New York — I mean, a woman has to work her way through school the best she can — so what I need is quickly to have one of you please put this color rinse in my hair for my job tomorrow." Finally, she found the plastic bottle of hair elixir she was looking for in her bag. "Thank God I found it. That would have been a disaster if I left it in New York . . .

"Oh, and I also am looking for, starting this weekend, a furnished apartment somewhere convenient, or a bed-and-breakfast, or something, a guest room . . . the local hotel is closed for remodeling!"

This was indeed true. The Ashville Inn, established in 1774, had just closed until the Fourth of July. It was being refurbished in time for the annual Rose Festival.

Before anyone else could, Bonnie took the bottle of color rinse and led Florida to her chair in the salon. (She wouldn't admit until weeks later how terrified she was to touch Florida's hair for fear of overprocessing it or doing anything that might upset the famous, million-dollar mane.)

Conversation centered on where Florida might live while she was in Ashville.

The inn really was the best place, but it was closed. There was a motel on the other side of town, but it was not very attractive. A place for transients and "one-night, more like one-hour stands, you know what I mean? I mean of course you don't know, what am I saying?" Bonnie said.

No one had ever seen her interacting so nervously with anyone. It was fun to watch.

"You could stay at my house," said Francie. "Praise the Lord, my teenage boy, Tony, would think his old mother was finally good for something — you know how teenagers are — if I brought you home." She didn't mention that Tony had a poster-size photo of Florida in a swimsuit on his bedroom wall.

Florida, her head in Bonnie's nervous hands, thanked Francie for the kind praise.

When a host of other ideas were exhausted, Mrs. Brown said: "I have a spare room and you'd be welcome to it." She couldn't believe the words had come out of her mouth!

No one else could either. Bonnie was so stunned by Mrs. Brown's audacity that she nearly dropped the bottle with Florida's hair color. Duly noted, reprimand Mrs. Brown later.

The supermodel sat forward in Bonnie's chair, her hair still soaking in bottle color, and craned her swan-like neck in Mrs. Brown's direction. "Do you really have a spare room, Mrs. Brown? Oh, I'd love to see it when we're done here."

"It isn't really ready to be seen; it needs some sprucing up," Mrs. Brown said. "I'm done here by seven, and if you give me about an hour I'll go home and clean up a bit and then please come by around eight?"

"I have to get back to New York tonight; it's at least a four-hour drive," Florida said. "Bonnie, would you mind if Mrs. Brown took me round to see the room when you're done with my color?" Bonnie leaned in to Florida's ear and whispered: "You don't have to be so kind, dear. Our old Mrs. Brown is a tough bird. You can say no and not waste your time."

Florida whispered back: "I may only be a haphazardly educated college senior, *dear,* but I, too, am a tough bird who can make her own decisions and rarely wastes her time."

Freud said anatomy is destiny? Maybe hair is, too, or hair salons.

If looks could kill, Mrs. Brown would have been six feet under, dead and buried, when she went off in Florida Noble's emerald-green Jaguar convertible, leaving her co-workers aghast, their mouths open, but for once in their lives with nothing to say — for now.

CHAPTER 13

The first things Florida noticed at Mrs. Brown's house were the smells of wood polish, strong tea, geraniums in their pots, the cat food, and, as Mrs. Brown went through the place opening windows, the brackish scents from the Fogg River nearby.

The bright overhead kitchen light made her squint. The kitchen table was so clean it practically sparkled. Instead of precious decorator color in the living room it was instead a wash of grays and browns. The dignity of the unremarkable pieces of furniture and the surprise of one: a light-color wood hutch with handsomely carved details.

A glass-paneled door opened to a narrow hall, where she saw two doors leading to two small rooms. To the left was Mrs. Brown's bedroom, to the right was a bathroom. Upstairs was a spare bedroom for Florida, if she liked it. They climbed the narrow stairs, Florida's high heels F-sharp on the red oak staircase. Mrs. Brown opened the door to the spare room and gestured for Florida to have a look.

The white blinds were drawn, the walls were papered in a kind of forest green, the bed was covered with a camel-colored corduroy spread, on top of which was an aged teddy bear with a sad, bemused expression that suggested he'd lost his best friend, or his best friend's balloon, a long time ago. Three small hooked rugs covered a spotted-pattern linoleum floor, and a maple desk with a maple chair and a brass lamp with a yellow-white shade completed the room. On the bookshelf was a football with several signatures, a Webster's dictionary, and an atlas.

"You are welcome to stay here while you finish school," Mrs. Brown said.

Florida entered. Santo jumped on the bed and raised his chin for Florida to pet.

"I'd love it," Florida told Mrs. Brown. "I feel at home already. I promise I won't be a pest — I'll stay out of your kitchen and in my room because I'll have so much studying to do — but Lord knows I'd rather be here so cozy and all and not in some hotel or apartment alone. Solitude is one thing, and very good for you sometimes, but being alone is quite another thing."

137

Returning to the kitchen Mrs. Brown put the teakettle on and opened the tin of Scandinavian butter cookies. There were a few left.

Florida, all legs and arms, sat at the kitchen table and stared at the cookies. "For every bite I'll lose a booking," she said, laughing.

"Booking?"

"A modeling job, they're called bookings," she explained.

Mrs. Brown nodded.

Florida smiled. She sat back, sipping her tea. The butter cookie she was eating was certainly the most delicious thing she'd ever had, and Santo in her lap the softest, sweetest cat. She felt so comfortable in her own skin tonight, which unfortunately was rare, even for such highly paid skin. The thought of what her friends would say, or the press, if they saw these humble digs, never entered her mind. The little lady with hands callused from manual labor at whose table she sat was kindness and courtesy personified. That is all that mattered.

"About money, Mrs. Brown. How is, say, two hundred and fifty dollars a week for, well, we'd better do the room through the summer term just in case I have to get an extension on my work or anything . . . so that would be —" She looked in her bag for her phone, putting a green leather notebook, folded pieces of paper, a lipstick in a gold case, and a pair of sunglasses on the table until she found her phone. Florida clicked away on the phone's calendar-calculator and counted the weeks — nineteen weeks. "Four thousand and seven hundred and fifty dollars. But let's say an even five thousand dollars, okay?"

It was a tremendous sum and would almost pay for her dress! Mrs. Brown was speechless.

"You're right," Florida said, misunderstanding her silence. "I'd be paying much more at the Ashville Inn, rooms there are two hundred a night. Seven fifty a week is more accurate."

"No," Mrs. Brown exclaimed.

"Five hundred?"

"No, no . . . that isn't what I meant. I mean, even two hundred and fifty is too much. I couldn't accept that."

Florida laughed. "Oh, Mrs. Brown, but it isn't. Not for what I am getting. And not for what I am used to paying at hotels these days, like the Ritz in Paris, the Four Seasons in New York, the Berkeley and Claridge's in London, the Sunset Tower in L.A."

Florida continued: "Even bed-and-breakfasts are charging over three hundred dollars a night in places like Vermont or the Sonoma Valley. . . . I'm just so grateful to have met you. There are no coincidences, are there? Isn't life wonderful when you get out of the way and just let it unfold?"

She didn't know what to say. They settled on two hundred and fifty dollars a week. Mrs. Brown wouldn't accept more. "What do you like for breakfast? I will make sure it is in the house," she said when she had regained her composure.

Florida Noble wrote Mrs. Brown a check in the amount of one thousand dollars as a deposit on the room.

Mrs. Brown said a deposit wasn't necessary.

Florida insisted, saying she wanted to do things the "big city way," and then left, thanking Mrs. Brown profusely and making her gilded way back to New York, promising to return in five days' time, on Sunday night.

CHAPTER 14

"Florida Noble and the cleaning lady! I mean, *Florida Noble and a cleaning woman!* What's the world coming to? We can't let this happen!" Francie declared the next morning.

It was Cinderella Central at Bonnie's Beauty Salon, and the news of the supermodel taking a room at Emilia Brown's house wasn't going down without envy and comment.

Fortunately, Mrs. Brown was not there to hear this. She was running errands for Bonnie.

"Bonnie, you should pay old Brown cow less while Florida is bunking with her," Hillie said emphatically. "She is making a fortune thanks to you. It's because of you she met Florida. She owes you some commission. That's how real estate works."

Bonnie decided she would try to remain neutral. Although she, too, was envious of

Mrs. Brown's inexplicable good fortune, she also was shrewd enough to realize that she should stay on her cleaning lady's good side. This would assure that Florida Noble returned to her salon, and often, during her time in Ashville.

"Nice things happen to good people," Bonnie said, perched at the cash register, counting her receipts. "Mrs. Brown is a hard worker who asks for very little."

"Oh, please," Francie said over her shoulder while she washed hair combs in her sink, "she is a manipulative little backstabber. She stole Florida right out from under us. My mother always said, 'Watch out for those little brown wrens,' course she meant they'd steal your husband, but whatever, she was right. Nowadays, they'll steal your job. And besides, what is she going to do with the money? She doesn't have a family to feed and we do."

Bonnie shot her a look that said that it was time to change the subject. But Francie continued.

"I give it one night, if she can last that long," Francie said. "One night in Brown's dull shithole, and that supermodel — honey, I don't care how much charity is on her brain — will be running for the hills. I'd make up your guest room, Bonnie, and be ready."

Meanwhile, Mrs. Brown, oblivious to the nattering chorus back at the salon, was finishing up Bonnie's shopping — paper towels, lemon-scented dishwashing liquid — and had proceeded to the dry cleaners. After having exchanged pleasantries with the proprietor, Vladimir Brzezinski — Vladimir had been one of Mrs. Brown's classmates at the Ashville High School — she was walking along Main Street with Bonnie's sweaters and pants in plastic wrapping when something new caught her eye.

Off Main Street in Ashville was a string of narrow streets with late-nineteenth-century three- or four-story brick buildings with offices, storefronts, and apartments. In some buildings, there were loft spaces that the more artistic constituency from the nearby college leased for working space.

A white sign with a red striped border got her attention. FOXBROWN & BROTHERS, it said and in smaller print, Mrs. Brown couldn't read the smaller print from Main Street so she took a detour and went closer.

FOXBROWN & BROTHERS FINANCIAL ADVISERS. Mrs. Brown was struck by the name, of course, it being hers and her best friend and neighbor's Mrs. Fox's. Financial advisers, she thought. Is this an omen?

She had missed the article a few weeks ago in the *Ashville Bulletin* about the Fox-brown agency opening here. Three brothers, from New York, who summered at their grandmother's "farm" nearby, had thought they'd leave the Big Apple and try their luck in Rhode Island (where the taxes were so much less than in New York).

So far, only one brother, the youngest, had actually managed to relocate from the city. Inside the office sat Stewart Foxbrown, tall, late thirties, wiry, preppy, a mop of brown hair, club tie, and pink button-down.

There wasn't much business today, or any time so far.

Stewart spent his days playing solitaire on his computer and checking Bloomberg for money's latest news. At night, he was pursuing a love affair with Mr. Jack Daniel's. Rising to refill his coffee mug, he noticed Mrs. Brown at the window.

A live one! He opened the door. "Hello, ma'am," he said, "need some financial advice?"

"How much?" Mrs. Brown asked.

"How much?" Stewart repeated. "How much for what?"

"For financial advice?" Mrs. Brown asked.

"It's free," Stewart said. Alas, this wasn't

144

a savvy investor at his door but a novice. Still, business was business, and business was better than boredom. "And if you decide to invest with us, we take commission on what you buy and sell."

The lady seemed puzzled.

It was chilly with the door open. "Why don't you come in and we can discuss it further," Stewart said.

Mrs. Brown hesitated. Stewart stepped out into the alley and held the door for her. It would be impolite to decline such a gentlemanly gesture, so she stepped inside.

"I have to get back to the beauty parlor where I work," Mrs. Brown said, resting Bonnie's dry cleaning and shopping on a wood bench next to the office door.

She noticed that this fellow wasn't wearing a wedding ring. If he was single, she might suggest he come by the beauty parlor to meet some of the beauticians who were unmarried. Just as swiftly as this thought came to her, it was dismissed. What if he was as nice as he seemed on first impression? She'd be doing him a disservice.

Stewart gestured for her to sit in the leather-and-wood chair across from his desk. "What are your financial goals Mrs. . . . ?" He waited for her name.

"Mrs. Brown," Mrs. Brown answered.

"What are my financial goals?" She paused. "To save enough money to buy . . ." She hesitated. Should she confide in this man, who, despite his endearing appearance — the mess of hair, the pink shirt riding up over his belt — was a total stranger, let alone a man?

"It usually helps if I know everything," Stewart said. This was true, and he also was curious. Except for the clerk at the liquor store, Mrs. Brown might be the only other human he talked to today.

Mrs. Brown told Stewart everything about her dress, about going to New York for the first time ever, that it would be nearly an eight-thousand-dollar event, more money than she had ever imagined spending on anything . . . until she got to the end, saying: "So I have a thousand dollars in my bag. What can you do for me?"

Stewart, who indeed was a man, didn't of course know how best to respond to Mrs. Brown's story. So he offered the basics: "If you invest the money for a year, you might be able to earn five percent, maybe, probably less. But whatever the earning, it will be more than you'd get if you leave it in the bank."

Mrs. Brown didn't want to wait a year. "What if I give it to you for six months?"

"Well, then, you still will earn more than in a savings account at a bank. We will invest in a diversity of companies," Stewart said, explaining what that meant.

Her next question was one of the most uncharacteristic things she had ever said: "What about speculating?"

Stewart cleared his throat. "Speculate? With a thousand dollars. Well, let's see . . ."

Needy as he was for both business and something to do, his inherent sense of decency prevailed. "I cannot suggest a stock for you to speculate in, ma'am. I might have some ideas, but I think only if you really have money to burn should you ever gamble on a stock, or on a horse or anything else people gamble on."

But Mrs. Brown wasn't dissuaded. An instinct, she had: "By any chance is there anything called Santo" — the name of her beloved cat — "I could buy stock in?"

"I don't know, ma'am, let's see," Stewart said, entering the name in his computer and hoping for Mrs. Brown's sake that nothing was found. But, lo and behold, there was a Santo Eco, selling today for $23.45.

"Seems it has risen about two dollars a day since last week. Why don't we just Google it here and see what the business of Santo Eco is. I always hate it when you find

147

out it isn't good for people, or it makes weapons or something . . ."

Mrs. Brown wouldn't want that either.

"Now, this Santo," Stewart said, reading professorially from his computer screen, "produces a variety of high-tech sorts of fabrics, including . . . It makes artificial flowers that when put in a vase with regular tap water supposedly can radiate enough heat to warm a room of upwards of three hundred square feet. Wow, that's amazing."

Actually, it sounded crazy, but Mrs. Brown overlooked that.

"I will take a thousand dollars' worth," she said, opening her pocketbook.

CHAPTER 15

Florida Noble telephoned that Friday to say she expected to arrive at Mrs. Brown's around seven o'clock Sunday evening.

Anxiously, Mrs. Brown prepared, and while she prepared she tried not to over-think the many ways that having a boarder, let alone this very special boarder, could go wrong. She focused instead on the domestic details she could control. She dusted and redusted Florida's room. She washed the bed linen that had been on a shelf in a closet and dressed the bed. She replaced the boyish corduroy bedspread with a blue and white piece of cotton she had owned for years, and, to give it weight, she sewed a sturdy one-inch hem around its edges. She bought hyacinths for Florida's room and made fresh lemonade.

In an unexpected gesture of support and kindness, Bonnie lent her an air conditioner. "Just in case summer comes overnight and it gets hot in her room," Bonnie said. "Those row houses like yours get so stuffy, don't they?"

One of Solomon Aquilino's barbers had installed the AC that morning.

Alice, meanwhile, was points elsewhere, helping chaperone the fifth-grade on an overnight trip to a teaching farm in Putney, Vermont. She wasn't expected back until tomorrow. Besides that, Alice wasn't sure if she was looking forward to meeting Florida. A person who smiled as much as Florida did in photographs was suspicious, as far as Alice was concerned.

Any confidence Mrs. Brown might have had regarding her star boarder was rattled when she overheard the beauticians at Bonnie's placing bets on how long Florida would last at her house — two days, one day, one night, no night were some of the wagers, twenty dollars apiece.

What concerned Mrs. Brown most was that her place had only one bathroom, and a humble one at that, without, as they call it in the decorating magazines, a "vanity," a sink with a big countertop and a mirror with Hollywood dressing room lighting to do one's makeup.

"But really, Mrs. Brown, it isn't going to be a problem," Florida had said when she first saw the house. "I grew up sharing a bathroom with five male cousins when I lived with my grandmother. This will be the Ritz compared to that."

Around three on Sunday, the telephone rang. It was Florida Noble calling on a cell phone, the connection rather fuzzy as she was talking on speaker in her car, saying she would be arriving early.

"And I'm never early, Mrs. Brown, I mean never — terrible defect of character of mine always being hopelessly late — I think maybe I should send out a press release. I know some haters who would consider this big news!"

Mrs. Brown didn't quite follow.

"So I figure I will be there by six and I'd love to take you out for dinner when I get there — please," Florida said. "What's your favorite restaurant in Ashville? Will you make a reservation? Say for seven o'clock?"

Mrs. Brown didn't have a favorite restaurant. As we know, she rarely, if ever, ate out. Besides keeping to her budget, she was brought up believing that, except on special occasions like wedding anniversaries and Valentine's Day, you wouldn't go to restaurants when you had a perfectly decent kitchen at home.

"But I don't have a favorite restaurant,

151

Miss Noble. Wouldn't you like to eat here your first night? Won't you want to unpack? I can make something simple. In fact, I was planning on it."

A home-cooked meal sounded like paradise. "If it is no fuss, Mrs. Brown? That would be wonderful. I rarely eat at home — anyone's home. Always on the run, always on the go . . . never really getting anywhere. And please, Mrs. Brown?"

"Yes?"

"Call me Florida? All my friends do."

"Of course, Florida," Mrs. Brown said. "And please call me Emilia."

Florida hesitated. You could hear the road through her phone. If she called her new friend and landlady by her first name, then who would be her Mrs. Brown, the kindly and good soul who from the moment they met had become such a soothing presence in her life?

What's in a name? (A lot.) "Okay, Mrs. Brown," Florida said. "I'll see you around six, Emilia."

CHAPTER 16

The dinner Mrs. Brown prepared was tomatoes in salted olive oil, soda muffins she had made in the morning, and a paprika chicken she put in the oven at 5:30.

Around 6:30 she was letting Santo out for some fresh air in the fenced-in area at the back of her house when she became aware of someone crouched behind a fern tree.

Of course she was frightened. But Ashville is a small town. For better or worse, you come to recognize people by their shapes and the casts of their shadows, or their gaits, before you even see their faces.

"What are you doing, Tony?" Mrs. Brown asked.

Her trespasser presented himself, his head bowed. This raggedy-looking teenager about six feet tall with scraggly brown hair, pale complexion, dark brown, sad puppy eyes, who was dressed in blue jeans and a faded pink T-shirt with a palm tree on the front and the wording MAUI WOW-IE, was Francie's son.

"Tony, what's going on?" Mrs. Brown asked. She knew Tony to be a sweet enough kid.

"Is Florida Noble here?"

"Excuse me?"

"Florida Noble?" Tony repeated. "My mother said she was coming to live with you today. Ohmigod, Mrs. Brown, she's so beautiful I have to meet her. *Please!* She's the fiercest of all the supermodels . . ."

Fiercest? Like tigers? Should she be concerned?

"You know, coolest. Hottest. Most *fabulous* . . ."

Mrs. Brown told Tony to come inside. Have some lemonade before she sent him home.

"I mean that commercial she did for Dolce and Gabbana, that's the fiercest thing she's ever done," Tony enthused. "Don't you think so, Mrs. Brown?"

She explained she hadn't seen it but indulged him. "Why don't you give me a synopsis?"

Which Tony did, in great detail, not taking a breath: "Here is Florida in the backseat of a black Bentley — do you think she'll drive a Bentley in Ashville, Mrs. Brown? — she's

154

sipping a cup of tea in a dainty china cup driving up some fancy street in New York looking in all the store windows until she gets to Dolce and Gabbana, where the car stops. Wearing just his chauffeur's suit jacket and pants but no shirt, the driver, played by one of the fiercest, most ripped male models in the world, opens the door for her and she gets out all legs first in this tight skirt to go into the Dolce and Gabbana store . . ."

They heard the sound of a car door on the street, and here was Florida Noble, in white jeans, a black T-shirt, a navy blue cashmere cardigan sweater, and brown alligator high heels, ringing the doorbell.

Mrs. Brown greeted her. Florida swept in apologizing for the way she looked. "I didn't do my face today," she said, following Mrs. Brown to the kitchen. "Does one's skin good to not wear makeup for a day or two. Au naturel . . . And I'm so sorry that I'm an hour late. I really thought I'd be early."

Tony was frozen, utterly awed.

It wasn't the first time a teenager had been dumbstruck in her presence. "Hello," Florida said, her voice purring, extending her hand to Tony. "I'm Florida."

Tony could barely shake her hand, his was trembling so much.

"Love your T-shirt," Florida said, and winked.

Mrs. Brown thought Tony might faint.

Santo played the peacock next. He jumped on the kitchen table, tail curled, elongating his neck for Florida to caress. Mrs. Brown shooed Santo off, but Florida scooped him up in her arms. "I love cats," she said. "He's no problem."

Tony was so jealous of Mrs. Brown's ratty old cat.

"Where are your suitcases?" Mrs. Brown asked. "Tony will get them for you, won't you, Tony?"

OMG would he.

Florida handed Tony the keys to her Jaguar convertible. Did life get any better than this? Maybe if he took the car for a spin over to the 7-Eleven where some of his pals would be hanging out? Otherwise, without proof, they would never believe him. Then he knew what to do! He'd have old Mrs. Brown — who wasn't anything like his mother had described, in fact, she was kind of cool and her house was really "vintage," meaning a good thing — take a picture with his phone of him and Florida. Asking Florida to take a selfie seemed brazen, in Mrs. Brown's house.

He got the suitcases. He'd be cool. Try

not to make Florida think he was stalking her was his reasoning.

"Cute kid," Florida said when he was out of the room. "Is he a relative?"

Mrs. Brown explained he was the son of one of the women who worked at Bonnie's Beauty Salon, and how she'd found him hiding, longing for a glimpse of her famous guest. Florida gladly posed for the photograph he wanted, and then Tony went home.

"Oh, Mrs. Brown," Florida said, sitting at the kitchen table and sipping from a glass of lemonade, Santo in her lap. "I am not famous. The things I advertise and the magazines I model for are the stars. I'm just a prop."

Florida thought she was being endearingly self-effacing and funny, but Mrs. Brown detected sadness in her voice. She responded with a motherly look.

"Everything okay?"

"Just tired is all," Florida said.

"We can eat now, if you're hungry," Mrs. Brown said. "Then you can unpack and get settled."

Since Florida had a 9:00 appointment with her academic adviser in the morning, this was a perfect plan.

CHAPTER 17

"Do not even think of picking up that broom or making the coffee without telling me everything, absolutely everything, that happened last night from the minute Florida Noble arrived," Bonnie insisted when Mrs. Brown got to work just after 7:00 the next morning.

Bonnie was already in her office, on her yoga mat, Omming away, chanting for money. The minute she heard Mrs. Brown's key in the door, she was off her mat and in her face wanting all the news, the biggest scoop in Ashville today.

"What time did she get there? Did she really spend the night? Was she driving the Jaguar? Who did she talk to on the phone? What television did she watch before she went to sleep? What did she have for dinner? *Excuse me,* and what was she wearing? How was her hair? The makeup was what?"

It isn't that she was opposed to it, but gossiping wasn't Mrs. Brown's forte. Bonnie pressed her nonetheless.

"Okay, relax. Start with what she was wearing," Bonnie said, drinking some kind of seafoam-green vegetable panacea from a plastic bottle.

Mrs. Brown, pouring water into the coffeemaker, described Florida's outfit to the best of her ability, the white jeans, the navy blue sweater, and the alligator heels.

"How high? One-inch, two-inch, three-inch, four inches, five, more, and she drove in them? Whose where they?"

"They were her shoes. Who else's?"

What an odd question.

And what a clueless, pathetic answer, Bonnie thought. "I meant the designer. Who designed the shoes?"

Mrs. Brown didn't know who the designer was, but she assumed, like the wonderful black dress and jacket she was saving up for, that anything she liked — and she had liked Florida's shoes — had to have come from Oscar de la Renta.

"Oscar de la Renta," she told Bonnie. "I think the shoes were made by Oscar de la Renta," Mrs. Brown said, finding her sponges and duster.

"Oscar de la Renta? Really?" Bonnie said, fixing her makeup in the mirror near the cash register.

Mrs. Brown dusted.

"Now listen, Mrs. Brown, just a word or two of caution for you today," Bonnie said. "It's about the other girls when they get here. I think they are, well, I think you should know that they are jealous of you . . . how's that for a twist? . . . because you've landed Florida Noble at your house while she is in Ashville."

For "a fun look" she said would "perk up" her day, Bonnie drew a beauty mark, a perfect little dark brown spot above the right corner of her upper lip. As she drew, she continued:

"Just gird your loins, Mrs. Brown, they might not be too friendly today. But I'll keep my eye out. You know, sweetie, I've always got your back."

CHAPTER 18

Mrs. Brown did feel a decided chill from her co-workers, even colder than usual. Although they were dying to ask her about Florida Noble, they'd agree to subsist on Tony's report via his mother.

Mrs. Brown survived the big chill with her innate grace. When a reporter from the *Ashville Bulletin* showed up wanting to interview her about what it was like finding herself landlady to one of the most beautiful people in the world, she declined.

Francie, however, followed the reporter to the door and was about to e-mail from her phone to the reporter's the photograph Mrs. Brown took of Florida and Tony last night.

To Mrs. Brown's amazement, Bonnie interrupted. She was getting quite fed up with the negative ways of the mean girls in her employ, and it remained in her best interest to be on the right side of Florida Noble. Besides, with Florida's endorsement of Mrs. Brown, she had begun to see her cleaning lady in a whole new light. Quoting copyright law that may or may not have been correct but sure sounded accurate, Bonnie said that the photograph could not be used without permission of the photographer, Mrs. Brown, and a signed release from Florida Noble.

Mrs. Brown shook her head no when the reporter asked if it was okay to use the picture.

Francie was furious. She'd have to do something to retaliate.

Mrs. Brown, on the other hand, was feeling on top of the world, meaning closer to her dress. Running some errands for Bonnie that afternoon, she decided to pass by Foxbrown & Brothers to see how her investment was doing.

Stewart Foxbrown hadn't noticed when Mrs. Brown entered his storefront brokerage. As was his wont, he was lost in his computer playing solitaire. Mrs. Brown cleared her throat. He didn't hear her. She did so again, and still he did not look up.

"Mr. Foxbrown," she said, and startled the broker.

"Oh, my goodness, Mrs. Brown, how long have you been standing there?" he asked.

"Just thought I'd pass by and see how my

162

investment is doing?"

"Hmmm . . . I don't know . . . I actually haven't . . ." He switched programs on the computer, then looked up. "What was the name of the stock again? Oh, that's right, Santo, named for your canary . . ."

"My cat . . ."

A pause.

"Is your cat unwell, Mrs. Brown?"

"My cat is fine."

"How's your canary?"

"I don't have a canary!" Mrs. Brown exclaimed.

The stockbroker's bonhomie tumbled. He grimaced. "Well, good thing Santo your cat is doing well because — Maybe you'd better sit down, Mrs. Brown, there's bad news." Stewart rose from his seat and went around his desk to clear a chair of golfing magazines so Mrs. Brown could sit. "How do I say this? Oh, Christ, I hate it when this happens . . ."

"What has happened?"

"Well," Stewart said, "your investment in Santo kind of isn't."

"Kind of isn't?"

"Hold on," Mr. Foxbrown said, "let me just look something up here."

He fiddled with his computer while Mrs. Brown froze.

163

"Now, let's see here. Yup, blasted! Wow, that was fast, from one week to the next. Seems an investigation has been launched into Santo revolving around trademark and patent infringement and the result is the stock has" — he hesitated before continuing — "gone down, I am afraid."

She felt faint. Shame burned inside her. *How could I have been so stupid as to invest my money in the stock market? What kind of idiot is run by wishful thinking like this?*

"How down?" Mrs. Brown asked.

"Let's see," Stewart said, putting figures into his calculator. "Your stock is worth right now if you were to sell . . . $179. I'm sorry, Mrs. Brown. It may come back up after the investigation is resolved."

"How long will that take?" she asked, thinking maybe a couple of weeks or perhaps as much as a month.

"Usually in such cases about a year, or two."

"What can I do?"

Stewart Foxbrown shook his head. "There's nothing you can do, I'm afraid, except wait. I certainly wouldn't advise selling. And," he said, returning to his computer solitaire game, "if it is any consolation, think about someone like Warren Buffett or even Donald Trump; they've been where you're at a thousand times and always manage to bounce back. Try to think positive, Mrs. Brown. Courage. What's that plaque on the Christopher Columbus statue over there in the town green say? 'Sail on.' We must when the blue chips are down sail on, sail on. This is what makes America so great."

Chapter 19

Coming straight home from Bonnie's, Mrs. Brown knocked on Mrs. Fox's door. She needed to talk to her best friend Sarah.

Mrs. Brown was so flustered and upset by losing her investment — so deeply ashamed of having succumbed to such folly — it took what seemed an eternity before she realized that Mrs. Fox was not there but away in Vancouver, and that the light she saw was the pearl-white glow from Alice's laptop.

Alice hadn't heard Mrs. Brown knocking on the door. Instead of correcting papers and preparing her day plan for teaching tomorrow, she was in deep reverie, on her headphones, listening to her music, her favorite orange blossom candle filling the place with just the right amount of fragrant bite and sweet, and answering questions for a "style quiz" posted on a favorite website. Silly but engaging questions that you were supposed to answer with the first thing that came to mind:

Q. How would your friends describe your style? (*Answer: Tomboy chic.*)

Q. What do you wear on a fat day? (*A. Baggy black T-shirt.*)

Q. What's always in your bag? (*A. Keys, phone, lighter, piece of rose quartz for good luck.*)

Q. Do you have a beauty secret? (*A. Sex. Or, almond oil for winter moisturizer; rose water in summer.*)

Q. If you could change one thing about your appearance, what would it be? (*A. Be taller.*)

Q. What style advice do you give your friends if they ask? (*Less is more.*)

Q. What's the most treasured item in your wardrobe? (*A. Black motorcycle boots.*)

Q. It's a hot date night, what do you wear? (*A. Black jeans, black tank top, black high-heel strappy sandals or boots depending on the season, black pearl stud in one ear and a white one in the other.*)

Q. If you were stranded on a desert island, what would your essentials be? (*A. Music.*)

Q. Yes or no to a nip and a tuck? (*A. Ask me in twenty years.*)

Q. If you were the fashion police for the

day, what would you ban? (*A. The fash-ion police.*)

Q. What's your guilty pleasure? (*A. Girl bubble baths, music, scented candles.*)

Q. If you could give a dinner party and invite up to twelve people, living or dead, fact or fictional, who would they be? (*A. Scout Finch, Cleopatra, Chrissie Hynde, Rihanna, Mother Teresa, Serena Williams, Sean Penn — don't ask — Stevie Nicks, Donald Duck, Karl Lagerfeld, Lena Dunham, my grandmother . . .*)

Q. What are you proudest of? (*A. Not freaking out in Ashville.*)

Q. What are you least proud of? (*A. Being too judgmental.*)

Q. What would you eat for your last supper? (*A. Tuna casserole.*)

Alice's casserole, it can be noted, went right to Milo's heart that Saturday night in November, when she made it for him on their second date. Bless his heart, too, because instead of his preppy cords and khakis, he dressed for Alice, a pair of black jeans, motorcycle boots, a black T-shirt, and apparently no underwear, either briefs or boxers. Like a key in a Harley ignition, this roughrider look couldn't have pleased Alice more. Rural New England life was suddenly filling with big surprises. When she asked Milo where he got those clothes, he answered, with a seductive smile:

"Always look way in the back of a man's closet or chest of drawers; you never know what you'll find."

What Milo didn't mention was that his conservative boarding school teacher's mufti was in the trunk of his car. He'd changed into this outfit in the bathroom of a Friendly's restaurant en route so his students and colleagues wouldn't see him.

Alice might still be answering the "style quiz" questions if she hadn't decided it would be funny to take a "selfie" of herself answering the "style quiz" questions, and when she did she saw something that looked like a low-hanging cloud photo bombing her. But it wasn't a cloud. It was the view of the top of Mrs. Brown's head through the glass in the front door.

Mrs. Brown looked awfully upset. Alice had never seen her so undone. Mrs. Brown was one of those people, like swans in water, always calm above the surface. But you never see their feet paddling fast to stay afloat.

"Come in, Mrs. Brown, please come in," Alice said, holding the door for her landlady. "What's up? Want some tea? Coffee?"

Alice led Mrs. Brown to the kitchen. She put the kettle on. The moment Mrs. Brown sat down at the kitchen table, she couldn't stop the tears from dropping. She told Alice what had become of her speculation in the stock market.

"I'm a fool, I'm a fool, I'm a fool," Mrs. Brown said, her elbows on the table, her head low, her hands covering her eyes and her tears. "And what's worse is that I'm an old fool."

Alice didn't know what to do or say. If Mrs. Brown were one of her contemporaries, or one of her young students, she'd wait for them to finish crying and come up for air. Then she'd tell them everything was going to be okay.

Alice pulled her kitchen chair as close as she could to Mrs. Brown. She placed her left hand on Mrs. Brown's back, and her other hand on Mrs. Brown's hands, and she said:

"No, Mrs. Brown, you are not. You are not a fool."

"I am!"

"You're not!"

And back and forth like this until finally Mrs. Brown caught her breath.

"We'll figure this out," Alice said with a confidence she didn't recognize. She just

170

knew it was the right thing to say, and to believe.

"We will?"

"I promise you that all is well and all will be well. You've still got the rent money coming from Florida."

"That's right. I do, don't I?"

"Don't be embarrassed because you lost your investment. It happens to everyone. That's business. But you will still go to New York, you will get your dress, you'll find your way there and you'll find your way home and then you can wear your dress" — she paused — "whenever you want to. You'll have it."

"I will," said Mrs. Brown, some confidence returning.

"I can see it now in your closet. The most correct and the most beautiful dress in the world." Alice was surprised at how uncharacteristically optimistic she was sounding, even more surprised that she was actually beginning to believe it. Maybe the people who lose out in life are those who cling to the belief that something is impossible — rather than believing it's possible — no matter how extremely unlikely it appears.

Mrs. Brown exhaled. "You know, Alice, you remind me more and more of your grandmother. You're just as kind and good

171

as she." Her eyes filled again with tears, but tears brought by the permeating feeling of appreciation and gratitude, not tears caused by sorrow and regret.

Mrs. Brown cleared her throat. It seemed that she was going to say something else, perhaps confide a secret thought or two, when the telephone rang.

"Probably Granny," Alice said, getting up to answer the phone. "It's the time of day when she calls." The fact was that only Mrs. Fox, or a telemarketer, ever called on the landline. Everything else was text or mobile phone.

When Mrs. Fox heard that Mrs. Brown was right there, she asked to speak to her. Alice passed her the phone and listened as Mrs. Brown repeated what had happened with her speculation in the stock market. In a recent letter, she'd told Mrs. Fox about investing in the stock.

Mrs. Fox listened carefully. Instead of engaging directly with the problem, she offered something comforting.

"I think about us, Emilia," Mrs. Fox began, her voice low and quiet down the phone. "Maybe it's a generational thing, or geographic? We're small-town New England girls. We are the quiet, steady types," Mrs. Fox said. "We're the shovelers."

"You mean ducks, like the ones at the pond?" Mrs. Brown asked.

Mrs. Fox laughed. "Well, yes, shovelers are a type of duck. But what I mean is shovelers as in shoveling. We're New England girls just after World War Two. Keeping our mouths shut, never complaining, shoveling through the snow so everyone, not just our families, but everyone in the neighborhood, could get to school, to work, to the library, to church, remember?"

Mrs. Brown remembered the bleak winters. As hard as they could be, they were also cozy times staying indoors at home.

"I just wish sometimes, Emilia, well, sometimes you are *too* quiet," Mrs. Fox said. "Wouldn't it help to talk?"

But she wouldn't press Mrs. Brown, not tonight, or ever. She was friend, not interlocutor.

"I guess something will happen; it'll work out," Mrs. Brown said, and smiled. "If it is meant to be . . ."

"It will be," said Mrs. Fox, finishing her best friend's sentence. "Everything is going to be okay in the end. And if it's not okay, it isn't the end."

Mrs. Brown passed the telephone receiver to Alice.

"Okay, Granny, it's suppertime here. I'll

rustle something up for Mrs. Brown and me to eat."

"Alice, listen to me," Mrs. Fox said with all the seriousness at her command. "What do I always say? 'Blood makes you related. Loyalty makes you family.' Emilia is family. Make sure she doesn't get too sad. Keep your eye on her. Promise?"

"Come on, Granny — man . . ." Alice wasn't in the mood for a lecture. She'd begun to say something about how weird Mrs. Brown could be sometimes, and her grandmother should give Alice a break, that she was doing her best to be a good neighbor, but stopped herself just in time, before she hurt anyone's feelings. After all, Mrs. Brown was still sitting right there.

"Yes, yes, I promise you."

Besides, Mrs. Brown wasn't all that weird. She was just left over from the last century.

"I'm sorry. Yes, I promise. I promise that I will telephone my mother more often," Alice said, covering so that Mrs. Brown wouldn't suspect anything insulting had ever been intended.

"I promise, Granny!"

Chapter 20

Later that evening, Mrs. Brown sat at her kitchen table mending and sewing some of the pieces from the dry cleaners that she took in to earn extra money.

She was reinforcing some diamanté buttons on a black silk blouse that belonged to the wife of Ashville's only orthodontist, but Mrs. Brown's thoughts were only of this painful day. Thank God she had Alice to go to, and that she was able to talk to Mrs. Fox on the telephone.

Whatever Mrs. Brown did next about her dress had to be more wisely considered. How?

"Go forward," her inner voice told her.

She put down the sewing, rested her hands in her lap, and closed her eyes. The soothing cliché "where there's a will, there's a way" came to her and then morphed into something more visual. "Where there's a wall, there's a way." Mrs. Brown saw herself a little girl standing face-to-face with one of the stone walls you saw almost everywhere in the countryside in New England. Where was the best place to climb over? Where was a secret door? There it is, the gold knob! In her mind's eye just as she was reaching for the golden object she heard the sound of Santo rushing across the floor to greet Florida Noble.

Mrs. Brown opened her eyes.

It was just past 8:30, and Florida apologized if she was disturbing Mrs. Brown — she saw the sewing and mending piled on the kitchen table needing to get done — but would Mrs. Brown mind if she made a cup of tea — she carried her own special blend of curative herb tea in a silk sack in her pocketbook — and would Mrs. Brown care to join her in a cup?

"The basis of the tea is chamomile with a dab of hops, too; the chamomile rests the nervous system and the hops soothes the stomach," Florida said. "When I am in Paris there's a Chinese herbalist I always go see . . . Oh dear, listen to me."

Mrs. Brown got up to put on the kettle, but Florida stopped her. "You wait on people all day long." She ran the water from the tap into the kettle and joined Mrs. Brown at the table. Santo leapt into Florida's lap.

"Santo, get down," Mrs. Brown instructed the cat.

"Oh, please, it's okay, let him stay," Florida said.

Back in the city, any city — London, Paris, Milan, but especially New York, where Florida reigned supreme amongst the fashion set — very few people would have ever seen this unvarnished, down-to-earth side of the supermodel.

While her professional life was often complicated, and Florida had never won any Girl Scout awards for good behavior, her motives in Ashville were simple. Before her grandmother died five years ago, Florida had promised she would make something of herself beyond modeling.

"The flesh will wither," her grandmother had said, "but the soul will always grow if you nurture it, Florida."

She'd promised her grandmother that she would get her college degree even if it meant giving up lucrative modeling jobs. The more time passed, the worse Florida felt about not keeping her promise. But today, her first official day toward her finals and graduation, she had a sense of peace and satisfaction she hadn't known in a very long time.

"My mother's family are from Jamaica,"

Florida told Mrs. Brown as they drank their tea, "and they were all farmers. No one went to college and few even finished high school. My mother could sing and dance quite well. She became something of a showgirl and a celebrity in Kingston. That's where she met my father, who was a pilot with British Airways. He lived in London. They fell in love."

Mrs. Brown looked up from her sewing, stitching the torn inseam on the trousers of a green silk evening suit. "Are your parents in Jamaica or England?" she asked.

"They never married," Florida said, studying Mrs. Brown's face to see if it registered any disapproval.

It didn't. It wasn't Mrs. Brown's way to sit in judgment. The world was already tough enough. Too many judges and not enough juries. "I'm sure they would have if they could have," Mrs. Brown said, resting her hands again. They were hurting.

"I think they would have, too," Florida said. She fixed her herbal concoction and told Mrs. Brown her story. Her father was not only white, the color, especially of men, her grandmother most mistrusted, but was also married with a wife and four children living in England. Grandmother vehemently disapproved of her daughter having an affair with a married man. Then Florida was born. Her mother went to London to be nearer her father, hoping she could woo him away from his wife.

"My mother returned to Jamaica heartbroken. Her looks suffered and so did her health," Florida said. "She began to drink way too much. My grandmother and I really had to take care of her. She was like our child. Then, when I was twelve, she quit drinking."

Mr. Brown had liked his liquor. Mrs. Brown had prayed he would not drink so heavily. "How did your mother stop?" she asked Florida.

"She found God, Mrs. Brown, or a reasonable facsimile."

Mrs. Brown stiffened and Florida apologized.

"Oh, please forgive me, Mrs. Brown, I meant no disrespect to the Lord."

"None taken," Mrs. Brown said, and smiled. "It is just when you said that I saw an image of God Almighty coming out of a Xerox machine one after another, so fast . . ."

"Like dollar bills being printed?" Florida said, and laughed.

"Something like that," Mrs. Brown said.

"I have a tendency to be a bit irreverent,"

Florida said. "People were always telling me, especially when I was growing up, 'Florida, don't be funny.'"

Mrs. Brown smiled. "You know, that's something I often wonder about, why people tell each other not to be funny. Seems to me, in this crazy world, humor is the least one can offer."

"Amen," Florida responded. "I have a photo album with me in my room. I always travel with it. I'll go get it so you can see my relatives?"

"I'd like that," Mrs. Brown said.

Florida went to get the album. Santo followed her.

When she returned with the photo album, Florida said, "Mrs. Brown, may I ask about that hutch in the living room?"

"Of course. What about it?"

"It's really very beautiful," Florida said. "How old is it?"

Mrs. Brown didn't know precisely. "Well, it goes back several decades for sure. My father's father, who was born and raised here in Ashville, was in the Navy and stationed at one point in Venezuela . . . Let me see, how does the story go? It's been a long time since I've even thought about it."

Mrs. Brown got up from the kitchen table and walked to the hallway, where she could see the hutch in the living room.

"One night in a village outside Caracas, my grandfather and some of his shipmates were in the local pub when a young boy ran in frantically looking for a doctor, for anyone who could help; his older sister was sick. My grandfather volunteered to help. He followed the boy home and found that the young woman wasn't breathing well. She had developed pneumonia after some kind of respiratory infection. My grandfather was able to help, the young woman recovered just in time for her wedding two weeks later to the richest young man in their province, and her father gave my grandfather this hutch to thank him. My grandfather shipped it home, and it ended up with me after my parents died." Mrs. Brown paused. "It was always my mother's guess that it wasn't the hutch as much as something smuggled inside the hutch that made my grandfather so happy to have it."

"Forgive me if this sounds terribly tacky," Florida said, "but have you ever had the hutch appraised?"

"Oh, it isn't worth anything," Mrs. Brown said, and laughed. "And my mother and I looked for anything left hidden inside and never found it." She interpreted Florida's praise for the hutch as an attempt to make her feel more confident about her humble home. Compared to the wonderful houses and hotels Florida knew in her travels, this house must seem very shabby.

"I am not an expert on antiques by any means," Florida said, "but my interior designer in New York, his name is Jesse Carrier, has a great instinct about these things. I have a feeling he'd think your hutch is very valuable."

Mrs. Brown was flattered, but she knew the hutch wasn't a big deal. "It is getting late and I want to see your photo album," she said to change the subject.

"If you'll permit me, I'll take a few photographs for Jesse just in case he thinks it might be an important piece? He could show it to an appraiser. You never know. Like on the PBS show *Antiques Roadshow,* maybe you're living with a treasure."

Mrs. Brown really was embarrassed now. "I am living with a treasure." She smiled. "And that is you, dear."

Florida laughed. "Maybe we should get a second opinion?"

"About what?"

"About the hutch," Florida said.

"You make *hutch* sound like a medical issue, a second opinion," Mrs. Brown said, and laughed.

"I'll go ask Alice, if you don't mind?" Florida said. "Let me get her."

Before Mrs. Brown could answer, Florida was across the hall knocking on Alice's door.

When Alice saw her through the glass, she worried that there was something wrong with Mrs. Brown, a turn for the worse after their talk earlier tonight. What else could it be?

"She's okay," Florida said. "I just have an idea I wanted to get your support on."

Alice invited Florida in. They'd met before, of course, and chatted briefly on several occasions. Just neighborly stuff, exchanging pleasantries; Alice still wasn't entirely sure what to make of the supermodel. Florida really did smile a lot, as all models seem to do judging by their Instagrams. How could Alice trust anyone who smiled so much?

But there was something appealing about Florida nonetheless. And it wasn't just her beauty, which was remarkable even without makeup, or the cool clothes that everyone envied or the perfect hair or her delicious perfume, a mix of evergreen, fig, and white rose.

Florida's heart was in the right place. Alice was beginning to see this.

"So I figure if you'll come with me back

183

over to Mrs. Brown's and if you don't mind agreeing with me . . ."

"What a weird thing to say. Why would I mind agreeing with you?" Alice said.

Florida looked Alice in the eye, and smiled gently.

Apparently, Alice hadn't hidden her distrust as well as she thought she had. But Florida was used to people doubting her motives. It wasn't always personal, she decided. We're a world that tells people how important it is to succeed, while being suspicious of most anyone who does.

Her plan was this, Florida explained to Alice: Yes, she'd send photographs of the hutch to her decorator in New York, and yes, she thought the hutch was probably worth something and if no, it wasn't, she was going to buy it, anonymously, through her decorator, paying enough so Mrs. Brown could buy her dress, but he'd never let Mrs. Brown know. It would be a secret. A secret Alice also would need to keep.

"What do you think?" Florida asked.

Alice wasn't sure. "Why don't you just give her the money?"

"I can't," Florida said.

"Why?" Alice asked.

"You know why."

"Because she wouldn't accept it."

"Exactly," Florida said. "Come on, let's go back to Mrs. Brown before she gets suspicious we're plotting something."

"But we *are* plotting something!"

"Girl, lighten up."

The camaraderie felt good, and they laughed, stationed in the hallway between the two homes.

"But . . ." Alice began to say.

"But what?" Florida asked.

"Sometimes I think I get it, and then I don't," Alice began. "I mean, all this money that Mrs. Brown is saving for her dress that she could use to take a really cool vacation somewhere, or renovate her kitchen — I mean, who has linoleum like that anymore? — and then all the stress of her big trip to New York when she could shop online — like the rest of the world already does — or buy it vintage, online, if she wanted to save money, and bottom line . . . why this dress?"

Alice shook her head. "Sure, it's really well made, beautiful, the most proper suit dress in the world, but come on," she said. "She's as likely to wear it as she is an evening gown. Where *is* Mrs. Brown going to wear this dress, anyway? Really? She doesn't go anywhere. She's not running for office or anything, or even going to an office. Know what I mean?"

Florida's hand was on the doorknob to Mrs. Brown's place. "There's something very empowering when you do something that's really correct, or even wear something that's really correct."

Alice wasn't convinced. "You mean like people who dress up in their Sunday best for church. Do you think that makes them more religious, in the eyes of God?"

"I don't know if it makes them more religious, but probably the practice of dressing up renews their faith in the ritual of going to church on Sundays," Florida said. "And that's a good beginning."

She remembered something she'd read a while ago on a website she liked called PositivePrescription.com. "There was a study of a group of students at Harvard who always dressed up to take their exams. Suits and ties and dresses and jackets, that sort of thing," Florida said. "The members of the group that dressed up always did better on their exams than the students who didn't."

"But what test is Mrs. Brown taking?" Alice wondered.

"I've got a few ideas, but I don't know," Florida said. "Maybe it's still being written. Meanwhile, I think of Mrs. Brown as a butterfly. I know that sounds like a cliché, but really. A butterfly emerging from her cocoon after a long time in darkness."

CHAPTER 21

Florida's instincts were entirely correct. Based on the initial photographs she sent, her decorator agreed that the hutch probably was valuable, certainly way more valuable than Mrs. Brown ever guessed. He'd asked Florida for a few additional shots, close-ups of details and markings, and she'd sent them along immediately.

Only a few weeks later, through one of the antiques and furniture dealers the decorator had contacted, a buyer was found for Mrs. Brown's hutch. A month after that, on July 18, Mrs. Brown received a check for fifteen thousand dollars from the dealer, who had then sold the hutch — with a 50 percent markup on what he'd paid — to a man who ran a hedge fund in Greenwich, Connecticut.

"Imagine that, a gardener who wants to pay so much for my old hutch," Mrs. Brown said in jest to Alice. She knew perfectly well the only thing green about a hedge fund is the cash.

Alice didn't for a minute think a hedge fund guy had parted with all those coins for Mrs. Brown's old hutch. She'd texted Florida right away.

"Bullshit about the hedge fund dude, right? It's #GoodDeedInADirtyWorld."

"Actually, wrong! Happy to report!" Florida texted back, with three smiley faces for emphasis. "Isn't it great news?"

"I promise you can tell me the truth. I won't tell Mrs. Brown," Alice responded.

"I give you my word on the head of my firstborn — when my firstborn is born," Florida texted. *Truth xoxo.*

So Alice believed her. Well, the way Alice believed anything to be true. True until proven not true.

The day the check arrived, to Mrs. Brown's regret, Florida Noble wasn't there to celebrate. She was in New York City working. Starring in a commercial for a splashy new mobile phone that was being filmed on top of the Empire State Building. They were paying her a small fortune.

"I'm terrified of heights," Florida said when she left for the city that morning, "but money, especially a lot of money, somehow always calms my nerves."

When filming the commercial was completed, Florida would return to Ashville for her final two weeks at Guilford. Having Florida rent a room had been such a pleasure for Mrs. Brown. She'd miss her.

After the initial fuss and curiosity, the good people of Ashville and, even more important, their tween and teenage children, had relaxed and left Florida to come and go with utmost privacy. In fact, most had taken to amusingly asking "Florida who?" whenever her name was mentioned.

And here was the cobalt-blue parchment envelope with the fifteen-thousand-dollar check. All thanks to Florida Noble.

Mrs. Brown brought the envelope across the hall. "You open it, I am too nervous," she told Alice.

They sat at the kitchen table. After they'd taken their time to admire the envelope — as if it were a Picasso or some other masterpiece — Alice opened it with the precision of a surgeon, using a kitchen knife. She ceremoniously laid the check in front of Mrs. Brown.

Alice and Mrs. Brown were silent, just staring at the regal black ink on light, hopeful green paper from Citibank: $15,000.

"A fortune," Mrs. Brown said, nervous to touch the check.

The antiques dealer whose check was in the aforementioned blue envelope had included a note that thanked Mrs. Brown for selling the hutch. Made of tropical hardwoods, ash, and mahogany with inlays of imported Italian tiles, it was a 1922 work by a noted Venezuelan craftsman named Humberto Ricardo Garcia. The fact that it was signed by Don Humberto made it even more valuable, the dealer said.

A cranberry and walnut bread that Alice had just baked — she was still rehearsing recipes before she served them to Milo — waited on the kitchen table.

Alice spoke first. Now that the check had arrived, Mrs. Brown would soon set off to New York City.

"Mrs. Brown, um, well, there's just one thing I keep forgetting to ask you . . ."

Mrs. Brown answered before Alice finished.

"Absolutely, Alice, they do. I have telephoned Oscar de la Renta in New York City twice a month, on the first Monday of the month, and then the third Friday in the month, and each time someone has told me that they do. They have the dress and they have it in my size."

Alice reached across the table and rested her hand on Mrs. Brown's.

"Then isn't that amazing, Mrs. Brown? You're going to get your dress after all and have a nice little nest egg left over."

CHAPTER 22

Bonnie was reluctant to give Mrs. Brown any time off. On a rainy morning in early August, Mrs. Brown went to the beauty parlor to open up and found Bonnie already there, in her office, stretching on her yoga mat and howling, which, as Mrs. Brown knew, wasn't howling, it was chanting.

"I do not chant for things because God doesn't like that so I just chant for God's will and hope his will is to send me more money!" Bonnie explained.

Bonnie, on her mat with legs crossed, studied Mrs. Brown's face. "You look tired," she said.

"I'm sorry," Mrs. Brown responded. Whenever Bonnie said anything about her appearance, she always interpreted her meaning as: you're not looking smart enough to work in my beauty parlor today.

"What are you sorry about? Just make some coffee. I've had a horrible weekend. I woke up yesterday morning, and you know what I realized?"

"What?"

"I realized I was alone."

Mrs. Brown didn't quite understand her meaning at first. Bonnie lived alone — her grown son lived in Hartford, her daughter in Boston. Unless someone was sleeping over, how else would she wake up except alone?

"I mean really, really alone," Bonnie continued in the exaggerated, dramatic way she had. "I'm like an apple who falls off a tree. I roll around on the ground until I think it's time to get back on the tree, but then you can't. You're not a squirrel. You don't climb. And then the apple, me, realizes oh, my effing God, I am alone. So, so, so alone down here."

Mrs. Brown made the coffee while Bonnie went on about apples and apple trees, and then something about a big male poodle raising its leg on trees. Mrs. Brown tried to understand.

When the coffee was ready, Mrs. Brown prepared a mug for Bonnie the way she liked it, black with three Sweet'n Lows, and brought it to her.

"Bonnie, I'm hoping it'll be okay with you if I take a few days of vacation."

194

"Why? Since when have you gone on vacations?" Bonnie asked, her coffee mug in her hand. "You got a boyfriend all of a sudden? Well, I hope he is a better son of a bitch than the guy I've been seeing — oh, that's right, you know who he is. Thanks for keeping it our secret, honey. He stood me up Saturday night. Stood *me* up! Never called. And I made vegan! I goddamn chopped vegetables for days for the son of a bitch." Bonnie made a face, a little-girl oh, me, oh, my smile, to apologize for swearing.

People were always apologizing to Mrs. Brown for swearing in her presence, but no one actually ever stopped swearing. "I threw that vegan slop out and grilled myself a steak."

Mrs. Brown had no intention of telling Bonnie where she was going or why, but she tried to disclose in a general way the importance of taking a vacation this summer.

"I've learned so much from you, Bonnie," Mrs. Brown said, attempting to get what she wanted by flattering her narcissistic boss. "And one of the things I've learned is how important it is for a woman to take time to recharge her battery."

Bonnie, enthroned mission control on her stool by the cash register, swiveled and stared. She was flattered, but not persuaded.

"When do you want to go?"

Mrs. Brown said the first week of September.

"Sorry, not that week. It is the week after Labor Day and we are always very busy then, remember? Everyone's seen the new fashion magazines and they all want their new hairstyles. Old dogs, new tricks, Mrs. Brown."

Mrs. Brown proposed the week after that. Bonnie had a problem with that, too. In the end, Mrs. Brown was given just one day off.

"Wherever you are going, trust me, short trips are the best," Bonnie said, handing Mrs. Brown her empty coffee mug. "They cost you less money."

CHAPTER 23

It had been a summer of lilacs and roses, heat waves and thunderstorms in Ashville.

In mid-August, Florida had completed her studies at Guilford with great grades and accolades. After a tearful goodbye, she left Mrs. Brown's, although she would return, ten months later, to receive her diploma during Guilford's annual graduation ceremonies.

Finally, the time had come. Mrs. Brown's trip to New York City was tomorrow.

Alice was helping Mrs. Brown prepare.

Now that it was September Alice was back to work full-time. She'd stayed in Ashville to teach in her school's summer program — and to be near to Milo, while he ran the summer arts program at the boarding school where he taught.

Alice and Milo were having a wonderful time. Because it stayed light so late in the evenings, they often met midweek for picnics somewhere in the distance between them. They'd fallen in love, and their love was still so new, that they never had to talk about it. The feelings just were. No need for discussion, except where and when to meet next. If only love could always be that light.

Having conferred with her grandmother many times on the telephone over the course of the days leading up to Mrs. Brown's trip, Alice was determined tonight not to show how worried Mrs. Fox was, or for that matter how worried she was, about Mrs. Brown's maiden day in New York City.

Their concern was for the obvious. That Mrs. Brown had never been to New York City, its energy field more rage than romance. The city is a horse that throws you the minute it smells fear, and the first visit for anyone — even the most sophisticated traveler — is overwhelming.

As Mrs. Fox liked to remind Alice, she had been to New York quite a few times in her many years, usually a very exhausting day trip with her church group for a matinee of a Broadway show, a performance at Lincoln Center, an exhibition at the Metropolitan Museum, and then home to Ashville after midnight. The drive to Manhattan took at least four hours, and, even in the safety of a group of church friends, she was always rattled by something, whether it was the sirens, the traffic, or a painful situation she saw on the streets.

And if the city got to Mrs. Fox, so comparatively sophisticated, how would it affect Mrs. Brown?

Alice had spent a summer three years ago interning at a charter school in Harlem, and although it seemed, in memory, like it was only a matter of hours before she felt perfectly at home, out on the town in Manhattan and other boroughs — Brooklyn, the Bronx, and Queens — it was more like a month before she found her footing, and, truth be told, survival every day was a negotiation with the city beast.

How was Mrs. Brown going to cope when she entered the wild kingdom right off the train at Pennsylvania Station?

In conversations between Mrs. Fox and Alice, and in consultation with Mrs. Brown, a list of things to pack, remember, and do had been prepared and vetted many times over.

It was to this list, written on a pad of yellow legal paper, now on the kitchen table next to a small vase of pink Ashville roses cut from a bush outside the kitchen door, that Alice referred tonight:

"You've packed a bottle of water and

smelling salts in case you feel suddenly faint?" Alice asked, sitting at the table, Santo in her lap. She couldn't believe that in the twenty-first century she was discussing smelling salts, but her grandmother had insisted.

"I have them," Mrs. Brown said. "And by the way, I telephoned the store again this morning. The dress is there."

Alice checked this off the list.

"Read me the rest and I'll make sure I've done everything," Mrs. Brown said.

Alice cleared her throat and read: "Bus tickets from here to Westerly?"

"Check," Mrs. Brown answered.

"Train tickets to Pennsylvania Station, round trip, plus receipt to prove purchase, just in case?"

From a white canvas Rose Festival 2008 commemorative tote, bought at the Ashville Thrift Shop, Mrs. Brown produced a Ziploc bag. It held all the important documents for tomorrow, the bus and train tickets to New York and back, and a MetroCard that Alice had asked a friend in Manhattan to send her for Mrs. Brown to use on city buses.

"Next: address of the Oscar de la Renta store on Madison Avenue?"

Important phone numbers and addresses were written on a white unlined five-by-seven-inch index card. "Here it is," Mrs. Brown said, reading from the card, "772 Madison Avenue at Sixty-sixth Street."

"And you've got your cell phone and you've charged the battery?"

Mrs. Brown, who rarely used her mobile, nodded. She'd charged the phone.

Mrs. Brown had already memorized the directions but nonetheless read from the card where they were written: "Exit train and once inside Pennsylvania Station look for signs that say Seventh Avenue, not Eighth Avenue. Exit Pennsylvania Station on the Seventh Avenue side, which will be between Thirty-first and Thirty-third Streets, cross the avenue to West Thirty-second Street, then look for signs for the M4 bus which will take you up Madison Avenue. Watch out the windows of the bus for signs on the street corners and get off the bus between Sixty-fifth and Sixty-sixth Streets. You will be on the east side of the avenue. Walk north to Sixty-sixth Street and cross Madison Avenue to the northwest corner where the store is located at 772 Madison."

Alice pointed to the MetroCard. "Follow the little white arrows on the card when you insert it. Point it downward, as the arrows indicate. Or just ask the bus driver how it works," she advised. "Don't be shy, Mrs. Brown. You won't be the first person who has asked a New York City bus driver for assistance, believe me. And don't take it personally if when he or she answers they aren't especially polite. They don't do Ashville polite in New York."

Santo left Alice's lap for Mrs. Brown's.

"Now we should go over your travel itinerary again, just, well, just because," Alice said.

At 5:00 tomorrow morning, September 10, Mrs. Brown would leave her house and walk to the Ashville bus station, about twenty minutes away. At 5:40 she would board the bus for Westerly, getting in at 7:00. She would walk from the bus stop to the Westerly train station and wait for the 7:25 train to New York's Pennsylvania Station scheduled to arrive at 10:20. Exit Pennsylvania Station; walk to and find the M4 bus; and, assuming the bus was operating on a timely schedule, estimated time of arrival at the Oscar de la Renta boutique? 12:30 P.M.

"If not sooner," Mrs. Brown said.

"If not sooner." Alice smiled.

Next they discussed Mrs. Brown's return to Pennsylvania Station in time to catch the 7:50 P.M. train back to Westerly, which

202

would be much easier than getting to Oscar de la Renta because it had been decided Mrs. Brown would splurge and take a taxi back to the station. She would be carrying her dress, and a taxi promised more space than the helter-skelter crush of the bus, especially if it was crowded.

"To know which taxis are available and which aren't, just look to see if the On Duty sign is lit on the roof of the cab," Alice explained. "The majority of tourists don't know this is why so many empty taxis zoom past them. You'll see."

A few minutes past nine Alice got up from the kitchen table; it was time for her to go home. She repeated her promise to Mrs. Brown that she would feed Santo tomorrow.

Alice's heart ached, not in a sorrowful way, but with gratitude and appreciation. A lot of people only give lip service for wanting support. Mrs. Brown genuinely seemed to benefit from Alice's help, and it felt good to be useful.

"God, what can I say to Mrs. Brown that sounds right," Alice asked herself in that moment.

The words came.

"I hope you know, Mrs. Brown, that if I ever seemed not to understand why this trip is so important to you, I apologize. I appreciate and respect you so much. I'm so happy I've gotten to know firsthand why you're Granny's best friend."

Alice paused. "And my heart's with you all the way, Mrs. Brown. And you know it's not too late to change your mind. If you want, I can still come with you. I haven't missed a day of teaching since I started last year. I can call in sick. I get sick days. Even if you decide in the morning, just give me thirty minutes' advance notice and I'll be ready to go with you."

What Alice didn't say was that she had already put her go-to-the-city outfit at the foot of her bed and packed a handbag with everything she'd bring if Mrs. Brown needed her to come along at the last minute.

Mrs. Brown stood. She smiled. Looked into Alice's kind blue eyes. Quite uncharacteristically for someone so reserved, she opened her arms to embrace Alice, not the melodramatic way the women in Bonnie's beauty parlor did, or like the reality show wives on TV, all silly kisses and arms bruising the air with champagne glasses and expensive pocketbooks. But the way Mrs. Brown used to hug her mother, and the way Mrs. Brown's mother would return the embrace.

Alice's was a generation of huggers and shoulder bumpers, but the embrace surprised her nonetheless. As she returned the affection, in physical contact so close that she could smell the violet soap Mrs. Brown washed with, tears of worry, and of parting, which she didn't want Mrs. Brown to see, filled her eyes.

Real tears are contagious, and Mrs. Brown didn't escape. Her eyes filled with them, too. "I'm glad, Alice, that you don't think I'm silly," she said.

"I never did, Mrs. Brown," Alice said, wiping a tear from her eye. "Silly is the last thing you will ever be."

CHAPTER 24

Mrs. Brown was early to the bus depot, walking Ashville's village streets as if she, and she alone, were tasked with drawing back the night for the morning light.

She boarded the almost empty bus to Westerly, the driver gruff as rust, what you might expect of someone who drives too early for too long. It was hot, bubbling doubt — equal parts fear and shame — not tea or coffee that woke Mrs. Brown up. What was she doing? Who did she think she was?

She closed her eyes and saw her dress and the eventuality of owning it. Then her purpose and courage returned, and she was calmed.

Arriving in Westerly, Mrs. Brown walked the short distance to the train station. She bravely asked a complete stranger if she was standing on the right side of the tracks for the train to New York City. She was. Westerly, certainly compared to Ashville, was the nexus of all activity this morning. Noise. Trains announced on the loudspeakers. Security warnings. People yelling down their cell phones with what seemed like urgent details of what they ate for breakfast, or where they had parked the car.

The first train coming through was heading northeast to Boston. The sound was deafening for someone like Mrs. Brown, who was more familiar with sentimental trains in movies and on television than with trains racing up and down the Northeast Corridor.

Mrs. Brown was dressed in her standard uniform, her gray lighter-weight wool-blend trousers, a brown twinset — cardigan sweater and shell — and nondescript black loafer-style shoes with a small rise of heel. She was carrying her mother's favorite handbag, a black leather bean-shaped purse in a style that was popular in the 1950s. Inside was a small clipping, a photograph probably of what? Her dress, you'd suppose. She studied it. Smiled. Reached for a white handkerchief she'd sprayed this morning with a favorite rose scent that would remind her of home. She took it from her purse now and dabbed at her nose, inhaling, exhaling.

Breathe, she told herself. Breathe.

She could turn back. There was still time to be at Bonnie's by eleven. She would apologize. She'd say she finished early, that she didn't need the entire day off after all.

Who else was here, waiting for the train? What was their purpose in going to New York? On the bench next to her was a young man in a brown khaki cotton suit, blue shirt, and red necktie reading a salmon-colored newspaper, the *Financial Times;* she'd never seen this paper before. Were the headlines always so grim? WEEKLY JOBLESS CLAIMS RISE and FACTORY ORDERS FALL . . . WORLD BANK PRESIDENT WARNS EURO-PEAN LEADERS, a reminder that Mrs. Brown wasn't alone in her fears and concerns about financial security.

It's not too late to turn back and save your money, her inner voice cautioned. Go forward, a stronger voice said.

The train from Boston came speeding into view. Thundering until still, it had arrived at the platform forty-three seconds ahead of schedule. "New London will be next. . . . All aboard!"

She boarded the train, mindful of her footing. To Mrs. Brown, a travel novitiate, the train was as elegant as anything in an Agatha Christie novel. Hercule Poirot might appear at any moment with his knowing smile.

208

It was the plush seats, the handsome and attractively dressed businesspeople absorbed in their newspapers and digital tablets that all looked so luxurious.

Mrs. Brown was happy when she saw an empty seat near the window. She could look out and not miss any scenic Long Island Sound waterfront on the way to New York. She got comfortable, never letting go of her pocketbook fixed in her lap. Alice and Mrs. Fox had both warned her never to let her bag out of her sight. Mrs. Brown opened it and rummaged for a rumpled piece of notepaper. She'd written down the lines of a favorite prayer, one that always calmed her nerves, attributed to St. Francis of Assisi:

Lord, make me an instrument of your
    peace.
Where there is hatred, let me sow love.
Where there is injury, pardon.
Where there is doubt, faith.
Where there is despair, hope.
Where there is darkness, light.
Where there is sadness, joy.
O Divine Master, grant that I may not so
    much seek
To be consoled as to console;
To be understood as to understand;

To be loved, as to love.
For it is in giving that we receive.
It is in pardoning that we are pardoned,
It is in dying that we are born to eternal life.

"Amen," Mrs. Brown said aloud, and then noticed that the train conductor was standing over her.

"Goodness, I'm so sorry, I wasn't paying attention," she said, digging in her pocketbook for the Ziploc with her train ticket.

"Never need to apologize for praying," the conductor said, "not in America, ma'am."

In New London, then Old Saybrook, more passengers filled the car. The train barreled down the tracks toward New York City, such a foreign destination for Mrs. Brown but probably for everyone else on the train as familiar as their backyards.

In New Haven, a young woman Mrs. Brown guessed was about nineteen years old sat in the seat next to her, which until then had been empty. She had long wavy brown hair, wore blue jeans with high-heeled black suede pumps, and she carried a canvas bag not unlike Mrs. Brown's from the Ashville Rose Festival except hers said YALE UNIVERSITY. In the canvas bag the young woman found her iPad, and turned it on, glassy and bright as a Christmas light.

Mrs. Brown's attention went right to the pull quote on the page of the magazine the young woman was reading on her device. "She never knew what she wanted to be, but she did know the woman she wanted to become . . ."

The young woman noticed Mrs. Brown reading and turned her head and smiled. Mrs. Brown apologized for reading over her shoulder.

"Hey, no problem," the young woman said.

Mrs. Brown closed her eyes to rest and instead fell asleep. If you had asked her just fifteen minutes ago if she thought she would be able to sleep on the train, or should sleep on a train given security concerns, she would have certainly answered no. But the lulling of the train, the speeding view she saw of Long Island Sound from the window — the relief of being on time and finally on her journey — set her into a deep slumber with dreams in brief fragments: a desert, sands blowing, gray chiffon and dust, a young soldier with a homecoming smile, a flag; browning red and gold autumn leaves, teaberry-colored native Ashville roses on the banks of the fast-moving river . . .

CHAPTER 25

It was the most awful, frightening, disturbing smell. How was it that no one else minded?

On the platform at Pennsylvania Station, Mrs. Brown was overcome with the smells, of damp on rust, machine oils, honeyed roasting peanuts, and urine.

But here was the first sign she needed, to Seventh Avenue: this way. Mrs. Brown found her footing in the march toward that exit. She stopped at the sight of an escalator. She hadn't been on one in years. They don't have them in Ashville. They don't need them.

Mrs. Brown stood to the side while everyone else piled onto the escalator with the greatest of ease. Finally, when it was only herself left on the platform, she inched closer to the escalator. She bravely placed her right foot first and then the left and then up she went, heart first. She caught her breath before she would have to attempt getting off the ascending steel trap without stumbling. And mercifully she didn't stumble. She did just fine.

I've got to sit a minute and compose myself, Mrs. Brown thought. There wasn't any place to sit, at least not that she could see. The station was teeming with people crisscrossing in every direction, pulling suitcases on wheels or barking into cell phones, walking and texting, not looking where they were going, holding the other stranger responsible if they collided.

To her left, she was aware of a group of homeless men; everyone else moved in lines of transit, they moved in circles. One of the homeless men was singing, screaming is more accurate, his version of "I'll Be Seeing You." "I'll find you in the morning sun, and when the night is new. I'll be looking at the moon, but I'll be seeing you," the song that was written in 1938 by Sammy Fain. How that song brought back memories. It was her father's favorite, and she remembered him singing it to her mother, so long ago. Maybe hearing it, even in this tortured rendition, was some sign of protection for Mrs. Brown?

Instead of exiting on Seventh Avenue as preplanned, Mrs. Brown exited Pennsylvania Station on Eighth. It is an easy mistake to make. Whether it is a highway or a train station or a taxi's on duty/off duty signal, New York isn't famous for its accessible signage. It never was. Just ask any old-timer who remembers how tiny the highway signs for Idlewild Airport (now JFK) were back in the day. You scheduled your travel time to the airport to include missing the exit sign.

Mrs. Brown emerged in the noonday September sun on a baking hot sidewalk with people rushing every which way, the noise of it, the smell of it, from more roasting honey-sweet peanuts at one vendor's stand to the acid odor of fiery beef sizzling at another, curry to the south . . . this was suffocating. Then there was the babble, a ferocious roar she couldn't deny even with the cheeriest, greatest intentions for her day. If you factor in the seeming fact that one out of every three people was smoking a cigarette, exhaling eddies of smoke, then this must be what hell looks like, feels like, smells like, sounds like, if it isn't the real hell itself?

Maybe she hadn't fallen asleep on the train ride. Maybe she'd died, and here she was entering hell! Wouldn't that be justice for her folly! Mrs. Fox and Alice were right to have worried about her. She needed to sit. She needed to rest. She needed to go home! Mrs. Brown was beginning to panic. She saw a rat, a real rat, not a person, on the sidewalk. It skimmed a lady's leopard-print shoe; Mrs. Brown's heart raced. No benches to sit on? If there are benches in Ashville, how is it possible there are none here? Retreating to the nearest wall, she leaned against it, breathing heavily.

"Ma'am, you all right?"

She hadn't noticed the handsome young police officer standing next to her. When she saw him — his thick, wavy brown hair, square jaw, gray-green eyes, and olive complexion — she was shocked, not just by his protective presence but by how much he reminded her of another young man.

She was startled.

"Lady, you okay?" the officer asked.

There were tears in her eyes. She didn't understand. She must regain composure.

"I've never been to New York before. I just came out of the station and didn't know what to expect. I'd been warned, but even so, I never expected all this."

The officer studied her. "Ma'am, are you sure you are all right? Maybe I should call an ambulance. What is your name, ma'am?"

"My name is Mrs. Brown and I've come

to town." She heard her own rhyme. "To buy my dress."

The officer, Officer Pabon his badge said, took out a notepad. "What is your first name?" he asked.

"Mrs.," Mrs. Brown answered.

The officer smiled. "Christian first name, please. Mary? Nancy? Tiffany?"

Tiffany? There weren't any ladies in Ashville named Tiffany when Mrs. Brown was growing up. "Emilia," she said, "Emilia Brown from Ashville, Rhode Island."

"Okay, then. Where are you headed, Mrs. Brown, and do you need help with directions?"

A man wearing a skirt, leather vest, no shirt, combat boots, and his blood-orange-colored dyed hair cut in a dramatic Mohawk rushed past and winked at her. It was the strangest thing.

"It takes all kinds here, which is why I love New York," the officer said.

Uncharacteristically — Mrs. Brown confiding in a stranger? — she spilled all the details of her trip. She explained to the officer that she was headed to the Oscar de la Renta boutique on Madison Avenue and Sixty-sixth Street; she told him about Mrs. Groton; he'd heard of her and in fact had helped direct traffic on Fifth Avenue the

216

day of her funeral. Mrs. Brown explained to the young officer that she was looking for . . . She opened her handbag and found her handwritten itinerary crumpling by the hour from being examined by the minute, "the M4 bus that goes east on Thirty-second Street and north on Madison Avenue."

The policeman suggested it might be easier, because traffic was blocked on the East Side due to the summit at the United Nations of all the world's leaders, if she took a bus up Eighth Avenue, through Columbus Circle, and then got out at Sixty-fifth Street and took another bus east, through Central Park, to Madison Avenue, got out there, and walked one block to the boutique.

"If I had a squad car I'd run you up, which we aren't supposed to do, but I'm on foot today," the officer said. "But let me walk you to the bus," he said, which he did. A couple of minutes later, however, his radio went off and he was called elsewhere. He apologized for his sudden departure.

"You'll be fine today, Mrs. Brown, and I bet that dress is going to make you look like a million bucks. I hope you wear it someplace really great," the officer said and took off.

Mrs. Brown stood in silence amidst the

noise and city chaos. What was she feeling right now? It takes many nonnative New Yorkers years to describe those first impressions and sensations in the city, this opposing mix, like salt on sugar, of overly crowded and overly lonely.

When the bus finally came and she boarded, there was the challenge of exactly how to use the MetroCard that Alice had gotten for her. Fortunately the unsmiling bus driver put the card into the machine for her, her fare was paid, and her card returned. Mrs. Brown felt momentarily relieved. She even went so far as to take the popular theological leap to imagine that angels were here helping her today. And maybe there were. When a young man stood up and gave her his seat — her unpracticed stance was so wobbly it was making him nervous to think that she would fall — Mrs. Brown's confidence and trust were renewed. She regained her composure. She thanked the stranger and she was no longer feeling so alone. It was like starting her day in New York all over.

Sitting nearby were two medical students, one male, and one female, both in their mid to late twenties; the plastic badges around their necks affirmed their internships at the New York–Presbyterian Hospital. They were returning from a lecture and were discussing an article that, or so Mrs. Brown surmised, had been the subject of a recent class or lecture, and it seemed to be about. . . . Greta Garbo.

Male intern: Suppose that we began replacing your cells, one by one, with those of Greta Garbo at the age of thirty. Are you agreeable to this? Hypothetically, of course.

Female intern: Of course. Hypothetically. Okay. Sure. Go on.

Male intern: At the beginning of the experiment, the recipient of the cells would clearly be you . . .

Female intern: And at the end?

Male intern: And at the end it would clearly be Garbo . . .

Female intern: But what about the middle?

Male intern: Ah, yes, and what about the middle?

Female intern: Well?

Male intern: Well, it seems implausible to suggest that one can draw the line between the two — that any single cell could make all the difference between you and not-you.

Female intern: Then there is no answer

to the question of whether or not the person is me, and yet there is also no mystery involved. We know what happened.

Male intern: What happened?

Female intern: A self, it seems, is not all or nothing but the sort of thing that there can be more or less of.

Male intern: So the question then is, when does a person start to exist? When does a person cease to be?

Female intern: In the process of zygotes, because that is what we are discussing, although I'm beginning to suspect that perhaps we aren't, in terms of the zygote's cellular self-multiplication, there is no simple answer. It's all a matter of degrees.

Male intern: But the answer is simple.

Female intern: Is it?

Male intern: Yes, it is! Marry me!

Female intern: Puh-leeeze.

Male intern: You'll be my Garbo.

Female intern: I'd rather be alone.

Mrs. Brown smiled. "Bada bing!" the interns said in unison.

"Hey, lady," the bus driver called to Mrs. Brown, distracting her eavesdropping on this almost romantic comedy. "This is your

220

stop." She'd asked him to please tell her when they got there.

She thanked the bus driver and exited. Mrs. Brown cautiously held the railing. It was a tenuous endeavor at best.

Stepping onto the sidewalk was like turning on a switch, the roaring sound of the city and the noise in her ears — the noise! — and its vibration moving from her feet into her chest. Secondhand cigarette smoke and the smell of perfumes. The horrific majesty! So this is New York?

Yes, this is New York.

It was bewildering, to say the least. Every person she saw she felt she had seen before in a movie or television show, not that they were all glamorous, recognizable Hollywood star types, but characters, vivacious or gloomy, faces gray or faces painted and powdered . . .

Which way to the crosstown Sixty-fifth Street bus?

She was getting her bearings, looking left, looking right for a street sign, when an exotic creature, half pageant horse, half woman, came rushing toward her on stilts, or were they just very high-heeled shoes? Mrs. Brown was terrified at the prospect of being run down by this fortyish creature charging at her with a crown of brown shaggy hair and thick vampire-sharp bangs that covered almost all her face. When the woman got that much closer, Mrs. Brown saw her eyes, big brown saucers like the girls in those velvet paintings. These eyes were lined with thick clouds of black kohl. The woman wore a pencil-thin midcalf-length blue bouclé skirt and matching jacket with a wasp-tight waist, and when she was very close, Mrs. Brown saw her gold necklace, more like a bib, with dangling glassy stones and silver crosses.

"You! You? You! Are perfect," she declared, towering over Mrs. Brown.

Perfect?

"How would you like to go to a fashion show?"

"Excuse me? A fashion show?"

"Yes, to a fashion show. Everyone in New York wants to go to a fashion show this week — it's New York Fashion Week — and you, you, *you* are perfect."

"Am I?"

"Divine, dear. Just divine." The woman positively beamed.

"When?" Mrs. Brown asked.

"Now, right now, chop-chop, now; now in fact you are late."

The woman handed Mrs. Brown a ticket to the Robin Hood Is My Sister show —

she'd never heard of this label — on which was scribbled the seat number A17, and she said: "Go sit in my seat, and if anyone gives you a hard time just do this: turn a hundred and eighty degrees eastward, then westward, and say, 'Oh, well, Saint Laurent did it all forty years ago, didn't he?' and then do not say another word. Remain aloof. The secret of success in fashionland. Aloof!"

The woman paused. "Do you blog, dear?"

"Excuse me?"

"Never mind. Everyone is a critic. Everyone is an editor. Everyone is a fashion expert. Everyone has a blog. Blogs are the new black. Didn't you know? Haven't you heard? Where have you been, sweetie?"

She paused, but briefly. "Now, hurry up. Off you go to the fashion show. Go be me, the new me. My replacement." This creature out of *Alice's Adventures in Wonderland* studied Mrs. Brown's drab outfit of trousers and twinset, and said, "And if anyone, any of those little people who call themselves reporters, or bloggers, asks what the hell you are wearing — and what *are* you wearing? — just tell them it is vintage Comme des Garçons, but all you have to say is Comme, sounds like *comb,* for short. *Hurry!* You're in vintage Comme, and never forget it. The show is about to start. You're late.

Will last twenty minutes and then you can go back to going to wherever you are going. You *are* going somewhere, aren't you?"

Mrs. Brown nodded her head. "But where is this fashion show?"

The woman pointed west. When a lumbering delivery truck cleared out of the way, Mrs. Brown could see a portion of Lincoln Center — she recognized it from watching television shows on PBS. As she discovered, the spring fashion shows for next year were happening now, although it was fall — very confusing for the uninitiated — in a series of tents erected on the plaza of the legendary cultural center.

Just twenty minutes? Mrs. Brown wondered if she could spare the time. She checked her Timex watch, twisting its frayed brown band to see its face. It was 12:30. Should she risk it? If the show started at 12:30 and ended at 12:50, she could be on the bus at one o'clock. Why not?

It might be wonderful. The "shows" were something Florida had told her about in great detail on an evening when they were chatting in Ashville. Florida had described the fashion world's spectacle as "Kabuki on Judgment Day." A yearning to see pretty things overtook Mrs. Brown in that moment.

As if called by some preternatural queen bee into its hive, Mrs. Brown walked west, so plainly dressed, carrying her traveling things in a canvas tote, and entered the big tents with the best of them — the whippet-thin women who made torturous high heels look easier to ride than bucking broncos and the cheerful men in their dandiest suiting and a preponderance of peekaboo bare ankles, God knows why.

Everything that happened next happened very quickly.

It was as crowded here as it was at Pennsylvania Station. Fortunately, it smelt better. The people were like rare birds, different than the people on the bus or the pedestrians on the sidewalks. Here they were plumed in remarkable clothing, either extremely colorful or solidly black, and skinny all, walking on those high heels, storks and robins and parrots and sparrows in this tented aviary.

At the first of two checkpoints into the show, Mrs. Brown was asked to present her seat assignment, written on her ticket. She didn't know the fashion system even remotely well enough to understand the tremendous risk involved here, at least for a person with any modicum of pride and self-preservation. No one would hesitate, in fact they'd enjoy it, to toss her right out when it was discovered that she was not one of them, the intended, the anointed invitee.

Mrs. Brown had been given a ticket to a front-row seat. More tears have been shed over fashion shows' front rows than *placement* at dinner at Versailles. Front-row seats at fashion shows are no more transferable than the sun is in the solar system. It was only because Mrs. Brown was among the last to arrive — and had arrived when all the attention and all the paparazzi camera lights were focused on the entrance made by three sisters starring in a reality television show — that Mrs. Brown was able to sit without ejection by the show's organizers.

There was a program on her seat. In it was the list of "looks," fashion-speak for outfits on the runway, and the exotic names of the models, such as Spike, Sonny, Elektra, Li, and Comedy. "We were inspired by the idea of Pocahontas on a Russian oligarch's yacht," the designers wrote to explain their inspiration for the collection Mrs. Brown was about to see.

"The world is so full of a number of things, I'm sure we should all be happy as kings!" The designers' mission statement concluded with this Robert Louis Stevenson couplet from *A Child's Garden of Verses*.

By the way, the intended occupant of this seat, the force whom Mrs. Brown had encountered just minutes ago on the street, was Martha Monn, the veteran proprietress of a boutique in Texas fed up with the fashion system, by which she meant the designers she considered untalented and unoriginal, and by the giddy young bloggers, whom she felt paled compared to her own years of hard work in the fields of fashion, or the work of the established reporters and writers she considered her colleagues dating back to the era before fashion became the New Broadway.

Whether Martha Monn was right or wrong to let her feelings get the better of her doing her job, Mrs. Brown benefited. Here she was perched, possessed by expectation and wonder. There was a moment's calm before a new, great pushing and shoving erupted: a celebrity singer, dressed in a kind of high-fashion igloo — white pouf, white feathers, white fur, white veil, and a choker of motherly pearls — was escorted by a gang of burly security men to a front-row seat across the runway.

Mrs. Brown took notice of the ladies she was seated between. To her right was a skinny slip of a girl dressed like Raggedy Ann. If she was fourteen years old, she was a hundred. To her left was a woman of substance with one bit of whimsy added, a gigantic pair of black-frame eyeglasses with cobalt-blue lenses. Unbeknownst to Mrs. Brown, the young woman to her right was everyone's favorite blogging ingenue, looking a little long in the tooth after a late night and then an early breakfast at Barneys to introduce a new collection of pocketbooks. To Mrs. Brown's left was the esteemed fashion writer from one of France's leading newspapers.

The lights went out, throbbing calypso music started, chased by the sounds of a computer-generated remix of Leonard Bernstein's Mass — then Nelly's pop classic "Hot in Herre," so take off all your clothes — oh, my — and in an electrifying blaze of light came a parade of some of the youngest, skinniest, tallest women Mrs. Brown had ever seen in her life. If they were not so able-bodied, the thinness would have been repulsive, but instead there was jubilation. They wore flowing, embroidered, semiprecious-stone-encrusted, silky dresses in shades of purple, pewter gray, and dry-blood red bound and gathered with jeweled belts of matching fabric — it was the most extraordinary parade she had ever seen.

Was it great fashion? Were the clothes well made?

"Are you a blogger?" the writer from France asked.

Except Mrs. Brown heard, "Are you bothered?" and answered, "Yes, it is quite loud," which the writer heard as "Yes, and I'm quite proud," which she found most curious. Perhaps she was the mother of one of the designers?

It was the fashion show spectacle, and not just the clothes, that dazzled Mrs. Brown. The breathtakingly painted models stomping like championship thoroughbreds ferocious in heels, the blasts of flashing camera lights . . . it was as exhilarating as it was alarming.

Her heart beat fast, her ears hurt, her neck was sore from looking left and then right, keeping up with the jet pace on the catwalk.

Now the music was a remix of Bizet's *Carmen,* the Habanera aria and the Toreador Song both. The models marched one final time up and down. The impact of heels pounding on the runway trembled in her chest like bass drums and tubas do at a parade. When the models completed this final tour, the two young, skinny male designers of the collection appeared, waved rather anemically, and then disappeared.

Just then, a beautiful woman unlike any Mrs. Brown had ever seen, wearing a blue-and-white dress with a full pleated shirt, leapt to her feet and raced past Mrs. Brown, shadowed by two bodyguards trying to keep up. Mrs. Brown felt their breeze in her face.

"Ines Spring," the writer from France said. "The editor?"

Spring clothes? What did she say about spring clothes? Mrs. Brown wasn't sure what she'd heard or what was the correct response, so she smiled. A good smile covers a multitude of uncertainties, especially in a foreign land.

Although the music had stopped, and the romp of models on the runway was done, there still was an enormous amount of hubbub and noise as the thousand or so fashion faithful pushed toward the exit and the next show.

Dozens of people rushed up behind Mrs. Brown, so close. The next thing she knew she was swept up in a kind of massive, high-heeled conga line in fevered pursuit of the exit.

Mrs. Brown emerged from the tent into bright sunlight, like a chick popping out of an Easter egg. There were clusters of young Japanese women photographing other Japanese women, each dressed more outrageously than the next. Several of these women wore black plastic Minnie Mouse ears with Minnie's cotton, red and white polka dot bows — Disneyland's tiaras.

Where was she?

The only thing she recognized was daylight.

Mrs. Brown was struggling to get her bearings. Eventually she recognized she was in the courtyard at Lincoln Center, where she had entered.

No more detours, she told herself, if she was going to get to Oscar de la Renta.

Seeing a policewoman about a hundred feet away, she headed right to her and asked for directions to the bus stop. The policewoman pointed the way to Sixty-fifth Street.

At the bus stop, Mrs. Brown clutched her MetroCard. That melting pot she'd heard New York described as so many times was at a roiling boil. Young men walking little white dogs on jeweled leashes, women in indescribably tight stovepipe jeans and those high stiletto heels, people of all ages leashed to their phones, looking down, and nearly colliding.

By now a couple of teenagers and a young Marine also were waiting for the crosstown bus.

Finally, she saw the bus heading her way,

a lumbering lion magnificent to behold. Soon, very soon, Mrs. Brown would be arriving at Oscar de la Renta for her perfect black dress, touching it, putting it on, purchasing it for a sum of money so large it still weakened her to think of it.

The bus stopped, its door opened. Mrs. Brown climbed aboard, and this time when she fumbled with her MetroCard, figuring out which direction it went into the machine, it was the Marine who helped. He helped her again when the bus began to move east, bumping forward and sideways, and Mrs. Brown couldn't find her footing. The soldier put out his hand, she took it, and he helped her to the nearest vacant seat. He took position nearby, standing erect as the bus caught speed and thumped its way across town.

The teenagers who got on the bus at the same time couldn't believe this tableau. Random acts of kindness?

On the seat the soldier led her to, someone had left a copy of the morning's *New York Post.*

RATS AT WORLD TRADE CENTER was the headline. It was a story about union problems at the rebuilding site downtown.

If unremarked before she left Ashville, it most certainly had not gone unnoticed that

232

Mrs. Brown was traveling to New York on September 10, the day before the anniversary of the tragic attacks several years ago. This close proximity to the anniversary of September 11 had topped Alice's and Mrs. Fox's list of concerns for their friend's maiden trip to New York, but Mrs. Brown hadn't been deterred.

Mrs. Brown offered the newspaper to another passenger nearby, a pencil-thin man with a shaved head, a red bow tie, and a blue seersucker suit. He accepted the tabloid with a grunt.

"You new to this city, ma'am?" the Marine asked, his accent from one of our southern states.

"I am," Mrs. Brown said.

"Me, too, ma'am. On leave here on an overnight and then off to see my folks in Woodville."

"Woodville?" Mrs. Brown asked.

"Texas, ma'am, eastern part. I miss it so much."

The bus crossed through Central Park. At Fifth Avenue, the stately apartment buildings were even more imposing than Mrs. Brown remembered from the movies.

"You take care, ma'am," the soldier said, smiling at Mrs. Brown as if they were old friends.

"Your family will be so happy to see you," Mrs. Brown said.

He bowed his head. "Hope so, ma'am."

Another passenger, a handsome white-haired man carrying a cane with an elephant's head saluted the Marine. Smiling from ear to ear, the soldier exited the bus.

A few minutes later, the bus driver announced, "Madison Avenue! That's you, lady."

Mrs. Brown held her breath.

"Courage, child," the man with the cane called after Mrs. Brown as she exited the bus. "The best is still to come."

CHAPTER 26

Mrs. Brown tried to orient herself in the correct direction to walk to Oscar de la Renta. Which way was up?

Coming toward her was a petite lady with flowing lemon-yellow hair walking what looked like two clouds. In closer focus, they were revealed to be two perfectly coiffed white standard poodles. Everyone else on the sidewalk, except Mrs. Brown, seemed oblivious. How was that possible? How could anyone ever become accustomed to such spectacle? It would be like taking a rainbow for granted.

Mrs. Brown noticed that the street heading to her right had been cordoned off and the traffic redirected because a movie or television show was being filmed. Instead of current-issue automobiles parked along the sidewalks, there were cars from the 1950s, Plymouths, Pontiacs, Chevrolets, and Dodges, to name a few that Mrs. Brown recognized from her youth.

She'd never seen a movie being made. She joined the people who had queued up along the police cordon to watch. The man whom she guessed was the director was giving orders through a loudspeaker. He went quiet when a tall, slender woman wearing a midcalf-length mink coat — it was seventy-six degrees in New York today — and a gray hat with a sloping brim exited the apartment building on the south side of the street and got into a yellow Checker cab, the door held open by the doorman, played by an actor.

"Cut," the director yelled.

And then this was repeated, the actress going back into the building and out again.

"Cut," the director repeated. And the action was done over again.

"She's gained weight," the woman standing next to Mrs. Brown said.

"Who?" Mrs. Brown asked.

"She has," the woman said, naming the actress Mrs. Brown didn't recognize. "The camera puts on fifteen pounds," the woman huffed, and walked away.

"Cut! Okay, we've got it," the director said.

The crowd that had gathered to watch began to disperse. As it did, Mrs. Brown heard something surprising. She heard chirping and looked up. Sure enough, on a high branch in one of the skinny trees there was a bird's nest with a mother and two newborns. Although no one else seemed to notice or to care, the discovery delighted Mrs. Brown, and she lingered happily for a few minutes just to watch.

Good thing, too, because by looking up Mrs. Brown also noticed the street sign. It informed her that she was on Sixty-fourth Street, meaning that she had walked down, not up, Madison Avenue and was two blocks away from Oscar de la Renta. She took a long, deep breath and corrected her course.

Maybe it was just beginner's luck and she shouldn't jump to any Pollyanna conclusions, but still, so far, so good. Don't you think that she who conquers herself is greater than she who conquers a city?

Mrs. Brown couldn't wait until she got home tonight to Ashville and told everything, detail by detail, to Alice!

CHAPTER 27

Tears burned her eyes, and they came quickly. As much as she tried to stop them, as mortified as she was that she was crying in front of anyone, let alone a stranger, Mrs. Brown couldn't stop.

"But I" — she could barely speak, gasping for air — "but I telephoned only yesterday to make sure . . ." Mrs. Brown hadn't the voice to continue.

Yes, yes, of course, Oscar de la Renta boutiques still sold that style of dress, the goal of her pilgrimage, but it wasn't in stock here today. Perhaps there had been some confusion when she spoke with whomever she spoke with on the phone yesterday?

"I am so sorry, ma'am," the Oscar de la Renta salesperson said, trying to soothe Mrs. Brown.

Concerned that this frail lady might faint into a heap, the salesperson gently placed her arm behind Mrs. Brown's waist and helped her toward the back of the boutique and a gold-painted wood chair, the sort you see in ballrooms or Madison Avenue boutiques. Another salesperson got her a glass of water, but it shook so much in Mrs. Brown's hand that she gave it right back, spilling some of it in the process. This only caused her more unhappiness.

Surely this was an error. "I am asleep and this is a bad dream," she thought. But then it hit her again, her failure.

You know how she felt. That rapid sinking feeling in her stomach that Mrs. Brown had always gotten, since she was a child, when she did or thought she'd done something wrong. First came this fevered, branding shame — that dark soul fire of horrifying embarrassment.

What had happened? Where did she go wrong? She replayed everything that had happened since she got off the bus at Madison Avenue and Sixty-fifth Street. After a few minutes of magical distraction, she had gotten herself to Sixty-sixth Street and seen that the Oscar de la Renta boutique was across the avenue. She crossed with the light and froze for what seemed an eternity at the corner in front of the shop. Inside she could see a glowing immaculate showroom full of beautiful dresses.

She inched closer to the doors and prepared to enter, coaching herself, convincing herself to "go forward, Emilia, go forward."

When a handsome tan and blond woman of about fifty went through those doors, Mrs. Brown followed, propelled by a sudden bolt of confidence.

Mrs. Brown stood in the entrance. In which direction would she find her dress? In a bid for time to think, she busied herself looking at a nearby display of pocketbooks.

A slender woman in a navy blue suit dress appeared at Mrs. Brown's side.

"May I help you find something special today, ma'am?"

"Oh, yes," Mrs. Brown answered, finding her voice. "Very special." She described the dress she had come to buy.

That is when the sword fell on her happy day.

"Ah, yes, one of our most popular styles every season," the saleslady said. "Unfortunately, we do not have any in stock here. We're waiting for a new shipment. If you like I can check on the computer and see which of our boutiques might still have one — what size are you? I am guessing an eight? A ten? We can have it sent here for you to try."

"Today?" Mrs. Brown asked.

You might wonder if this trouble Mrs. Brown was encountering was some funny business going on in the shop, something snobby and snooty, the attitudes that have made Madison Avenue so famously forbidding. Maybe it's still like that at some places, but most of the posh shops on Madison Avenue have figured out it is wise not to rush to judge someone a disingenuous shopper just because she or he is dressed poorly.

Thanks, or no thanks, to the informal way Hollywood actors and Silicon Valley potentates dress — yoga clothes, jeans, sweats, baseball caps, and carrying Starbucks cups — you just never know anymore who is CEO of a billion-dollar Internet operation or a Hollywood mogul.

What salespeople look for is your handbag. Mrs. Brown's simple handbag, which had been her mother's, shaped like a kidney bean topped with a very subtle clasp, or styles very similar, had inspired in the past decade fashion house versions that sold for more money than Mrs. Brown earned in six months. That Mrs. Brown was carrying this bag, easily mistaken for something Gucci or Prada signified, correctly or incorrectly, that she might be a serious spender and not just some tourist who would waste the salespeople's time.

Mrs. Brown could barely breathe, taking in the full meaning of the unbelievable news that her dress was not in the store despite having called just the day before and been told otherwise.

"Can you really find my dress and get it here this afternoon?" Mrs. Brown asked.

"Let's go over to the computer, ma'am, and have a look."

Mrs. Brown followed the saleslady to the computer/cash register tucked discreetly out of sight of store traffic. Mrs. Brown waited as the saleslady searched.

"There's a size two in tangerine — probably not the color you are thinking — at our Bal Harbour store. Let's see, okay, here we go, got it. At our Beverly Hills boutique, size eight and size ten. If I contact them right now, the dresses should be here . . . by tomorrow afternoon."

"Tomorrow!" Mrs. Brown cried.

Tomorrow was too late. How was it possible to stay the night in New York? She didn't know anyone here. A hotel? She couldn't afford a hotel room. The money from selling the hutch — so much of it intended for her dress or put aside for taxes — hadn't made her rich, just lucky.

And now her luck had run out.

Weren't hotel rooms at least a thousand dollars a night in New York? She'd heard Bonnie talking about that the other day, or maybe it was Florida who mentioned something. And if there were cheaper hotels, how would she know, and then find her way to one, if it wasn't right nearby?

She panicked. "I cannot be here tomorrow, I can't stay in New York, I've got to leave. I've got to go home!"

Here is where the tears dropped.

The voice in her head: What a stupid, what a silly old woman I've been about all this. How could I think, how could I possibly imagine that I of all people should have this dress?

The saleslady was rightly concerned and genuinely empathetic. What could the matter be? Her regular customers never reacted so emotionally to being told the objects of their desire weren't in stock, or if they did, she wouldn't know; they popped a pill or took a drink, vodka in small red-capped Evian water bottles they carried in their purses. Something else must be going on with the hickory-stick lady.

She led Mrs. Brown to a chair near the dressing rooms and got her a glass of cold water — Fiji was the brand, very Madison Avenue. As she did, one of her colleagues who had been watching this exchange came and whispered in her ear.

"Word to the wise, sweetie. I think I saw a photo online today of this woman at one of the fashion shows sitting in the front row. We might be being punked. You know, goofed on, or it might even be that is artist Cindy Sherman doing one of her characters," she said. "Or what if this woman is a reporter trying to provoke us so she gets a good story? Or she is some clever oldster intending to get a lawsuit going by claiming age discrimination. We better cover ourselves. Stall this woman. Pretend you are trying other means to search for the dress."

The salesperson's right hand was firmly planted on her right hip now. She was growing more suspicious of Mrs. Brown by the second. "What does she want this dress so badly for anyway? Is she planning a murder and needs something to wear to the funeral? I saw that on *CSI* the other night. Really. The murderer went shopping before she committed the crime and then tried to use her shopping spree as her alibi." She nodded her head, agreeing with herself. "Beware, sweetie," she told her colleague. "I think your country mouse might be a rat."

Chapter 28

It so happened that the head of Oscar de la Renta's public relations team was at the Carlyle hotel a mere ten blocks north, at Seventy-sixth Street.

When the urgent text came through about the uncertain shopper's meltdown at the Madison Avenue boutique, the PR executive was delighted to have an excuse to bring to a quick close her lunch with a banker whose company was always on the lookout for fashion businesses to invest in. (And equally on the lookout for fashion parties to go to.)

This lunch, organized by a mutual friend, included one further agenda item, to see if they liked each other, liked each other enough to perhaps go to dinner some night. In New York parlance, it was a predate.

Rachel Ames stood and gave the man her hand to shake. He instead leaned in for a social kiss. Not wishing to embarrass him by pulling away and insisting on the hand-shake, Rachel kissed the fellow gently on his left and right cheeks. His expensively groomed facial hair looked just fine but was unpleasant on her lips, a lasting impression. She rushed off, saying, "Goodbye, yes, of course, hope so, see you soon," and headed to the Oscar de la Renta boutique. Looking over her shoulder before she left the Carlyle, she was not surprised to see that the fellow wasn't particularly crestfallen by her sudden departure. He was merrily tapping away on his phone.

On the street this glorious September afternoon, her lackluster luncheon "date" underlined Rachel's feelings about her single status. She wished she had it in her to fall in love and marry a successful businessman like the one she'd just lunched with. A girl's got to think about her future, she told herself and laughed, then stopped laughing. But this woman doesn't seem to think that way. Marry money and you earn it. Whether it was dealing with his eccentricity, adultery, aloofness, insane schedule, you name it, nearly every one of Rachel's friends who married a man for his towering finances eventually ended up in some kind of emotional descent, her spirit taxed by the alliance.

Still, though. There was that vacant feeling that crept up out of nowhere, and cast its long shadow. It came now. Usually it waited until she was back home alone, this lonesomeness that stalked her. Uninvited, haunting her especially after those seemingly happy dinners with friends in whatever was the latest happening restaurant, where one chattered merrily through the din about diets, doctors, new clothes, weekends, and vacations by the sea, or Aspen — Aspen in the summer was the rage this year — and the next wedding to which she and her friends were commanded. For all its vim and vigor, youth can be a lonely enterprise.

Rachel shook the gloom away by walking as quickly as she could down Madison Avenue, past lines of tourists outside the Whitney Museum (still on Madison before it moved downtown) and on line for the rainbow-colored macarons at Ladurée. Rachel Ames was all about work now.

"Where's the problem?" she asked briskly when she arrived at the boutique. The salesperson who had helped settle Mrs. Brown in the back of the shop led Rachel to her. Rachel would size up the problem and resolve it with dignity and speed. The troubling lady would be on her way in minutes.

247

Instead Rachel Ames was speechless when she saw Mrs. Brown sitting posture perfect on the little chair, looking so forlorn and out of place.

Despair in her eyes, her nerves frayed, Mrs. Brown looked up at this blond, beautiful icicle. It took a few moments before Rachel Ames and Mrs. Brown fully recognized each other from those many months ago when Mrs. Brown had helped inventory Millicent Groton's things.

Seeing Mrs. Brown was disorienting for Rachel. Something was wrong. Something was out of context. It was like coming home from work and finding that a bird has flown into your apartment through a window you left open that morning (it happens in the city). Along with the surprise, Rachel was genuinely pleased to see Mrs. Brown again.

Rachel explained that after finishing helping to settle Mrs. Groton's estate she'd gone to work for Oscar de la Renta. She knelt down so they were on the same level and took Mrs. Brown's hands in hers as if they were old friends.

And by this time tomorrow they would be.

CHAPTER 29

The two women, one old, and one young, sat talking in the store's elegant dressing room.

"Haven't you ever stayed awake at night wanting something and shivering from the shame of wanting it so much and fearing you'd never have it?"

The question touched Rachel's heart. "How did you know? How could you tell?"

Having seen how close Mrs. Brown was to collapse, Rachel had taken swift action. Her smartphone blazing, she dialed and e-mailed until she tracked down Mrs. Brown's dress at the Oscar de la Renta boutique in Beverly Hills. Rachel organized for the store manager there to send overnight to New York one dress size eight and another size ten, one of which would fit Mrs. Brown.

Rachel promised Mrs. Brown that the dresses would be here by noon, one at the latest. She did not say that she, and at her own expense — she didn't want to embarrass Mrs. Brown — was actually having one of the young staffers at the Beverly Hills boutique fly with the dresses on the next Delta flight and bring them to the store himself. Except for possible weather delays, there would be no margin for error.

The only things that shock anymore are random acts of kindness. In this regard Rachel Ames liked to be shocking. Doing good deeds in a dirty world renewed her. Rachel would treat Mrs. Brown as kindly as anyone ever had, if not more so.

"But I can't stay overnight in New York," Mrs. Brown had said. Anticipating that Mrs. Brown's worries would include the high cost of a New York hotel, let alone the frightening prospect of being alone in this strange monster of a city, Rachel invited Mrs. Brown to stay the night at her apartment just a few blocks away.

"I have a guest room that needs a guest," Rachel said.

Rachel's office would take care of changing Mrs. Brown's train reservations so she could leave Pennsylvania Station at the same time tomorrow night, with her dress safe and secure in her hands.

Mrs. Brown hesitated. Could she really

accept Rachel's hospitality? And she was worried. "But my job, I've got to go to work tomorrow."

"Is there anyone who can fill in for you?" Rachel asked. "Or can't you just call and say you are taking a personal day?"

Mrs. Brown wondered. She shook her head no.

Compared to Mrs. Brown, Rachel enjoyed so many privileges and a charmed life. She felt exceedingly grateful.

"Are you sure, Mrs. Brown? Won't you stay?"

Mrs. Brown thought more about it. "I'll do it. I'll stay. I have to. Thank you so much, Rachel, thank you so much," she said, though she was still uneasy about her decision. "I'd really like to go home with my dress. I'll telephone my neighbor who is taking care of my cat. She'll be so worried about where I am, what happened to me. You might have to get on the phone so she knows I've not been kidnapped by pirates . . ."

Rachel laughed.

"And I'll let my boss know, too, although I'm not looking forward to that call."

Once Rachel Ames had showered kindness on Mrs. Brown, the salespeople at the Oscar de la Renta boutique relaxed and gladly did the same. As for Rachel herself, there were many other things she could and should be doing this afternoon — it was Fashion Week, after all — but she could get to them later in the day or early evening. Besides, every once in a while it is a good idea to let your assistant fill in for you. It gives her, or him, an opportunity to mature and to learn and, at the same time, reminds your assistant why you have the big job and he or she doesn't — yet.

Rachel proposed that they continue their conversation over a cup of tea or coffee, maybe something to eat, at the Plaza Athénée hotel nearby on East Sixty-fourth Street.

Walking with Rachel down Madison Avenue, through this glamorous casbah, Mrs. Brown wondered what people thought, if they noticed them and thought about them at all. Such an unlikely duo: one woman who looked like she'd risen from the pages of a glittering fashion magazine and the other like someone who had never read one. Could they be mistaken for mother and daughter?

Arriving at the Plaza Athénée, Mrs. Brown marveled at the elegant good order of the place. Rachel led the way to her favorite corner table in the handsomely appointed bar/tea area of the hotel's restaurant. It was decorated in the Anglo-French style, with wood-paneled walls and thick velvet banquettes. Small recessed pink lightbulbs above each table cast a warm glow. The room was filled with well-dressed ladies and affluent-looking gentlemen of assorted ages, sizes, and nationalities.

"I do understand wanting a dress and fixating on it, saving for it. I think the desire for something feminine and beautiful binds all women together," Rachel said. "But what I do not understand is why this particular dress, Mrs. Brown?"

Mrs. Brown smiled.

Rachel continued. "I mean, for sure it is exquisitely tailored and chic and appropriate but" — she paused — "why not something more colorful, lighter, more feminine and more silky or frilly? Something most women in this day and age would say was the ideal feminine dress? Like a gown you'd wear on the red carpet, you know, something that you wouldn't wear to work. Or to church, to a funeral, to a board meeting, the sorts of places where Mrs. Groton always wore her suit? This is such a stately sort of dress, highly functional and useful, but not glam."

"Glam?" Mrs. Brown asked.

"Sorry, that's fashion-speak for glamorous." Rachel laughed. "Some fashion people use the word 'fabulous.' " She paused again, concerned that she sounded like a silly snob or a drag queen or worse, just so deeply superficial.

Mrs. Brown tried to explain. She would confide things to Rachel like you might to someone you've just met on a plane. Something about the anonymity of New York City empowered her. What you say here will not be judged, and it will not be repeated, or even if it is, it's of no consequence because no one knows you. The women Mrs. Brown worked for at the salon weren't interested — were they? — in anything she had to say. Mrs. Fox was a great friend, her best friend, and Alice was her new friend, but in the name of friendship, respecting each other's privacy and boundaries, much was left unsaid, too much perhaps sometimes.

"The feminine clothes you are talking about are party dresses, dresses for making a woman feel young and pretty," Mrs. Brown said, speaking slowly, holding the delicate Plaza Athénée teacup in the palms of her hands, feeling its warming comfort. "For me" — her voice caught — "for me," she continued, "what I think is feminine is . . ." Her voice drifted off.

"It's okay," Rachel said, "take your time."

"When we were inventorying Mrs. Groton's things and I saw her perfect black dress, this dress I've come for today, a dress I'd seen Mrs. Groton wear to functions in Ashville, the Rose Festival, the opening of the new hospital wing, in so many of her photographs in the Ashville newspapers . . . when you told me more about this style, and how most all the First Ladies in the past thirty years had a version of it in their wardrobes, I was overcome by the need for a dress like that of my own. I know it doesn't make any sense."

"I don't know that it doesn't make any sense, Mrs. Brown. I think maybe I'm beginning to understand how much sense it does make," Rachel said.

"Then when you gave me that book, *Mrs. 'Arris Goes to Paris,* well, I never read such a story," Mrs. Brown said. "It really put this idea in my head. Did you read it?"

Rachel shook her head. She hadn't.

"This Mrs. 'Arris isn't so different from me, you know. Only the times she lived in were different. It was right after World War Two. The war had drained the world of all joy and color. Everything was rubble. Bombs, blackouts, rationing, everything had been an everlasting mess, and for too many

255

years. Then one day Mrs. 'Arris discovers this bouquet, that's what the dress looked like to her, a huge bouquet of flowers. She sees the most beautiful dress hanging in one of her clients' closets. She reads the label. Christian Dior. What's that? She doesn't know, but never mind. She vows right there and then that no matter how much it will cost, or how long it takes her to save the money, that she will have a Christian Dior dress, too. And even if she never actually wore the dress — where was a cleaning lady going to wear such a fancy thing? — she wanted, like every woman, rich or poor, to live with something that beautiful and hopeful *in her closet* before she died . . ."

Her voice quieted. "Because the war was over. Everyone, including a cleaning lady, deserved beautiful feminine things to look at again."

A waiter brought a plate of tea sandwiches to their table. Rachel had insisted Mrs. Brown eat something.

"Although it was a very, as you would say, 'glam' dress, this Dior dress that Mrs. 'Arris wanted, a red-carpet dress, the story kept reminding me of the dress I'd seen in Mrs. Groton's closet," Mrs. Brown explained. "Maybe it wasn't typically feminine, in fact it's the total opposite of Mrs. 'Arris's dress,

256

but it's so womanly and so, well, it's strong. Tailored. Organized. Purposeful. What's the word I'm looking for?"

"Dutiful," Rachel suggested.

"Yes. Dutiful," Mrs. Brown said. She liked that word. "And I have a duty to perform, something I very much need — I want — to do."

Mrs. Brown seemed distant suddenly, as if she was seeing someone, something, in another room.

"I never went into business," Mrs. Brown said, back to telling Rachel her story. "I never went to college. After Mr. Brown died, I went to work. Spending my whole life cleaning up and sorting things out for other people. Most recently I'm working at Bonnie's salon, where the women act like girls, mean girls sometimes, but mostly silly girls."

"And hurtful, I'd imagine," said Rachel.

Mrs. Brown nodded in agreement. "Yes, they do hurt my feelings, a lot, but they don't deserve to be talked about in such a nice place as the Plaza Athénée."

When she was young, Mrs. Brown had always worn something pretty and feminine to church dances. Her mother made her dresses. "I started making my own clothes when I was first married to Mr. Brown.

Once a month our church had proper dances for the young marrieds, they don't anymore, and that is when I would gussy up, pleasing Mr. Brown. Oh, I remember a little blue and white polka dot number made with Egyptian cotton, a kind of a shirtdress with a belted waist and full skirt . . ." She felt sad thinking back. "Absent friends and absent family" — she smiled, trying to lighten things up — "not much we can do, is there?"

"No, there isn't," Rachel said. "You never . . ." But some instinct stopped her from asking Mrs. Brown if she had any children. "You never wanted to go to college?" she asked instead.

"Oh, sure I did. I thought about going to college a lot," Mrs. Brown said. "But as the years went on, as I got older, as . . . as things happened as they do in life . . ." She shrugged her shoulders. "I never got there. Maybe it's not too late? I finally got myself to New York. Then what's next? Harvard? Or Yale?"

They both laughed. "You know, the women I always found myself admiring, including how they dressed, weren't the movie stars and starlets, but always the women who went to college and then into business, or did important charities, like

258

Mrs. Groton. Women who, I don't know, acted like grown-ups when all the other adults were acting like children. Good, orderly, strong, confident . . . dutiful women. That's what I think femininity is."

It didn't seem the right time or place for Rachel to offer Mrs. Brown the fashion worldview that the frilly baby dolls, the streetwalkers, the leathers, the torn-butterfly and the peekaboo styles — and everything Cinderella at the ball — were expressions of a contemporary, post–feminist era celebration of sexuality and liberation.

"Ever since that day when I saw Mrs. Groton's suit dress, I knew I had to have one in my closet. I'll respect it, you see. And," said Mrs. Brown, her voice now a whisper, "and it will respect me."

Rachel realized that for Mrs. Brown, and for so many women at her income level, just scraping by with few if any luxuries, the experience of fine tailoring and everything it represents, not some trendy or sexy number, could be transforming.

Trendy and teenager styles were everywhere, but fine tailoring? It was the luxury that was out of reach, except for the affluent. Such elitism saddened Rachel. Normally she was so proud to be a part of the fashion industry. Did it really intend to diminish, and sometimes infantilize, women with low incomes and advancing years who didn't fit the profile of the perfect, glossy, well-off customers for their brands?

Why shouldn't Mrs. Brown own a suit dress like Mrs. Groton's?

Rachel assured Mrs. Brown that she understood completely. "In the novel, does Mrs. 'Arris get her dress?" she asked.

"She sure does," said Mrs. Brown, not mentioning that she hadn't actually finished reading the book just in case anything happened at the end that might undermine her determination to make this trip to New York.

With a graceful flourish of her right hand pantomiming signing an imaginary slip of paper, Rachel Ames indicated to the waiter that she would like the check.

"And so you shall have your dress, too," she promised Mrs. Brown.

CHAPTER 30

As Rachel and Mrs. Brown were leaving the hotel, a man Mrs. Brown thought was the spitting image of a young Marlon Brando rushed into the lobby and turned a sharp right.

But just as he turned toward the reception area — it is an intimately sized lobby, nothing cavernous like the Hilton hotel — his heart felt like it took off on a rapturous flight: Rachel Ames. He had seen her before, and it was alarm and delight, desire and reverence, all exploding together: a deep crush.

But as quickly as his heart rose when he saw her, it fell. Even though he ran his family's prosperous flooring business, the go-to firm for most of New York's top decorators and interior designers, he and Rachel occupied separate worlds. Even if he spoke to her, the possibility of a friendship, or more, developing between them was unlikely.

Hers was the Ivy League world of rarefied, white-collar financiers — the "one percent," as they've been dubbed. His world was more blue-collar. He was a man who worked with his hands, well, managed a team of others who worked with their hands; it had been quite some time since Anthony Bruno installed his family's flooring on a daily basis himself. But when there was a problem, mosaics and a perfect fit, for instance, he'd pitch right in.

The point was, other than wishing Rachel a good day when he saw her — her apartment was across the hall from a big job his company had done not long ago — he'd never attempted a conversation.

Part of that was New York's fault. In apartment buildings like Rachel's, Anthony and his men had to take the service elevator. You didn't mingle with the residents. If you did, the prickly ones always complained about it to the building's management, the management would chastise the decorator or contractor who had hired you, and then you were in trouble. Ask a resident out on a date? You'd never lay flooring in this building again.

But Anthony remembered one special morning. He was supervising his workers in the foyer of the aforementioned apartment. The front door was open because of some problem with the marble floor they were setting. Into the shared space, Rachel opened her front door. She was going to work, heading to the elevator, and he'd never forget it: she wore high, thin black heels, a tight navy blue skirt to the middle of her knees, and a crisp, white cotton blouse with just a hint of cleavage. Her skin was like the softest rose, her perfume just a hint of gardenia.

What Anthony didn't know was that he did not go unnoticed or forgotten. He was wearing pretty much what he was wearing now: a white shirt and a pair of khakis. When Rachel opened her front door that morning, she certainly wasn't expecting this on her way to work: the joy that flashes in you where intuition lives. Then your rational mind — or is it just your mother's voice in your head? — tells you to look for something wrong, to curb your enthusiasm, act a lady. Marry well.

But you couldn't miss the sparks between Rachel and Anthony this afternoon. Mrs. Brown certainly had noticed. The delight in Anthony's eyes and the smile on his face beamed across the lobby. Catching this energy, Rachel paused for a long moment and looked. Like a gazelle might when it encounters a potential mate, Rachel rose in stature, high at the shoulders. But then, her arms crossed her chest as if to protect her heart.

Mrs. Brown's motherly instinct was to promptly effect some exchange between the two young people.

"A friend of yours?" Mrs. Brown asked.

"No, not really," Rachel answered.

Anthony couldn't hear what Rachel was saying, but she was looking at him, and moving her lips, so he, thinking positively, imagined that she was saying something nice in his direction.

He crossed the lobby like a knight in summer khaki, his hand out to shake Rachel's.

"Anthony Bruno," he said.

Her mother always told her that it is the lady's place to extend her hand first, not the man's. Never mind. Rachel took Anthony's hand in hers. It was a good, strong handshake, warm and trustworthy, muscular, a couple of calluses, not fleshy or clammy.

"I am Rachel Ames, and this is . . . Oh, goodness, Mrs. Brown, I don't know your first name."

"Emilia Brown," she said, and extended her hand to Anthony.

"I remember you from . . ." Rachel and Anthony said at the same time. They laughed nervously.

"My family owns a flooring company. We had a job in the apartment across the hall from you."

She wasn't sure what to say. "Are you doing some work here in the hotel?" Rachel asked. When she was nervous, which she was, she could sound like a real ice princess.

A luggage cart with so many Louis Vuitton suitcases of various sizes they could fill a small store was wheeled past by a porter.

"Actually, I'm here to pick up the keys to a car. Not under the happiest of circumstances, however. A great client of my family's died and left me his 1970 Mercedes convertible," Anthony said. "His lawyer left the keys for me here because the car is in a garage around the corner," he explained. "It was one hell of a shock when I got that call. Oh, ma'am, excuse me for swearing."

Mrs. Brown took no offense.

"Hey, why don't you come with me for a ride?" Anthony said, seeing his chance to spend time with Rachel.

He was an enthusiastic fellow most of the time, but this sounded too enthusiastic, even to him. He tried to take the temperature down by acting a bit cooler.

"I mean, excuse me, you know, if you want?"

Mrs. Brown and Rachel exchanged glances, not knowing what to answer.

It wasn't in Anthony's constitution to hide his light for very long. "Or, tonight, even better, we can go to dinner if you like," he said.

The lobby bustled with people coming and going. An elderly guest in a wheelchair, young newlyweds on their honeymoon, string musicians carrying their instruments to set up in one of the reception rooms for a cocktail party, a nurse escorting to the elevator a woman whose head was wrapped in surgical gauze like a mummy, her nose red, her mouth puffed out, and her eyes black and blue.

This was an upsetting sight for Mrs. Brown, but Rachel explained that the cause was elective, not an accident. "She's had a face-lift of some sort today," Rachel said. She looked at her watch. "Four thirty. Time to go home after surgery."

Anthony pitched in. "That's right, ma'am," he told Mrs. Brown. "This neighborhood is filled with plastic surgery clinics, and if you are on the Upper East Side at this time of day, as many men as there are women, you'll always see people with their heads all wrapped up, looking like mummies, being escorted home or to a hotel . . ."

"Which is where some people prefer to recover for a day or two to not upset their families and loved ones with their frightening bandages. Not that I'd know firsthand — yet." Rachel laughed. "It's just that I live in the neighborhood." She paused. "How ridiculous I must sound." Rachel looked apologetically to Anthony.

Anthony smiled. "You don't sound ridiculous to me." He'd gone from steed to colt in love, and he was nearly blushing. "We just want you to know, ma'am, that you shouldn't be scared," he told Mrs. Brown. "That the bandages aren't bad news. They're good news. I think. It's proof of scientific progress." He laughed. "Or at least a sign of good news for the economy, people are spending their money. So will you ladies honor me and come for a ride in my new car? I mean, my old new car?"

Rachel was surprised when she heard herself saying yes.

"I think it is such a fun idea, especially because Mrs. Brown has never been to New York and what a great way to see everything, from a convertible on a beautiful night."

"Your first time in New York?" Anthony

exclaimed. "We must do this! There's a wonderful new restaurant in Harlem. It is almost impossible to get a table, but we did the flooring, so I think I can swing something."

Mrs. Brown wondered how to respond. A part of her wanted to explore the city and all its lights and glory. Another part told her that Rachel and Anthony were a love match and just an evening alone together now could lead to wedding bells in their future.

"Thank you so much, but I should stay in tonight. I am tired after a long day, and Rachel has been kind enough to let me spend the night," Mrs. Brown said. "You two should go, though. You must. I insist."

But Anthony felt so undeserving of Rachel, and Rachel felt so uncertain about Anthony despite the attraction, that they hemmed and they hawed and said things like "Oh, well, perhaps another night," and "Oh, yes, it's a busy week. Maybe when things slow down a bit." Mrs. Brown knew if she didn't change her mind, Rachel and Anthony might never see each other again.

"You've convinced me," Mrs. Brown said. "I would like nothing better than to see New York with you tonight."

CHAPTER 31

It was just past five that afternoon.

By the real estate standards of New York, where every square foot is worth a princely sum, Rachel's apartment was both simple and deluxe.

Located on East Seventy-fourth Street between Madison and Park Avenues, it was on the tenth floor of a doorman building, two apartments on the floor sharing a foyer and an elevator entrance.

Inside Rachel's apartment there was a long entrance hall and a black and white floor. The first thing Mrs. Brown noticed was the lush arrangement of white roses in a crystal vase on a mahogany credenza.

All the rooms in the apartment were off this reception hall: the living room, with two gray silk sofas and two blue and white upholstered chairs. The dining room, painted a high-gloss casino green with a round mahogany table and eight chairs with zebra-print needlepointed seats. The kitchen was L-shaped and not very large, a small table squeezed into the corner with a banquette for seating.

The bedrooms were at the other end of the hallway. There was a walk-in closet for Rachel's clothes, shoes, and bags, colorful as a paint box and big enough to be another bedroom.

"I'm going to dash down to my office and be back by seven to get ready for tonight," Rachel said after she showed Mrs. Brown the apartment and the guest room. "Here is my cell phone number. Call me with any questions, if you want something, or if you don't see how something works." Rachel scribbled her number on a pad embossed with her initials.

"You've really been too kind," said Mrs. Brown. Her eyes filled with tears.

Rachel said: "By the time you are on the train back to Ashville with your new dress tomorrow, I hope you will know that the kindness you speak of was entirely mutual. Meeting you, I mean, meeting you again was just what the doctor ordered."

Rachel paused. She took visual inventory of what Mrs. Brown was wearing. Since they were going to dinner at the Great Blue Heron, something was needed to perk up

Mrs. Brown's outfit.

It wasn't a problem to bring some Oscar de la Renta pieces home for her later, but no. That could hurt her feelings. As if Rachel was suggesting that Mrs. Brown was lacking or not belonging in some way.

Rachel remembered that she had just the thing, vintage Hermès scarves that her grandmother had given her before she died several years ago. This was a collection of colorful, sportif silk scarves the grande dame had worn when she was "motoring," as she called it, around Newport in the 1960s.

All it would take would be one Hermès scarf loosely tied at Mrs. Brown's collar and she'd look like a New England matron, the WASP way, never fancily dressed. The last of a breed that is resolutely suspicious of every expensive fabric except mink.

Rachel would introduce the scarf before dinner.

"Okay, Mrs. Brown, I'm off," she said. "Please rest and enjoy the apartment. We've got a big night ahead of us. And please feel free to use the telephone."

Rachel remembered that women of Mrs. Brown's generation had grown up at a time when long-distance telephoning was expensive.

271

"You'll get much better reception than you will with your cell phone. Don't worry about the cost," Rachel said. "I pay a flat monthly rate, and even if you talked until morning you won't exceed it."

In Rachel's guest room, Mrs. Brown sat enveloped in an enormously comfortable Queen Anne chair covered in a chintz field of faded cabbage roses.

There were two phone calls she needed to make right away. The first was to Alice, who would be worrying about her. The second was to Bonnie. Mrs. Brown could not predict how her boss would take the news that she was not coming to work tomorrow.

Let me not think about that for a few more minutes, she told herself. Let me just sit here and breathe in all this goodness.

What an extraordinary twelve hours! Don't people often say that their first trip to New York was like stepping into a movie, a movie about New York? That's certainly how Mrs. Brown felt this afternoon.

Mrs. Brown expected that for the rest of her life she would be deeply embarrassed when she remembered making a scene at the Oscar de la Renta boutique. But although she might always be embarrassed because of that, she wouldn't be ashamed. Her days of being so hard on herself were coming to a close. This trip had boosted her self-esteem tremendously.

Mrs. Brown sat in the chintz-covered Queen Anne chair, her feet up on the ottoman covered in the same fabric.

She closed her eyes. Images of her day sped by. The train ride, then Pennsylvania Station, the exotic fashion show at Lincoln Center, the good soldier on the bus. She saw her cat, Santo, waiting for her in Ashville, and Alice, and Mrs. Fox worrying about her far away in Vancouver. She remembered her husband, Mr. Brown. How much they had enjoyed their early married days, all embraces and companionship before his drinking went too far, then fighting about his drinking. Praying so hard that he'd stop. Her mother's voice, telling her to "pray with a feather not a pickax!" The only time Mr. Brown stopped drinking was when he died. He always said he wanted to be buried with a bottle of Old Grand-Dad, 114 barrel proof.

"Hell freezes over, and I know where I'm going it's going to be dark and cold, lovey, and I'm going to keep as comfortable as I can for as long as I can," he said. "Old Grand-Dad, 114 barrel proof. You won't forget?"

Mrs. Brown didn't forget. It was unlikely

that she ever would. Even though Mrs. Fox had offered to do it, she bought the bottle herself at Ashville's village liquor store and gave it to the undertaker to put in her husband's coffin.

Mrs. Brown fell asleep in Rachel's Queen Anne chair. It was unusual for her to nap like this during the daytime. Only if she was ill, with flu or a cold, might she sleep during the day.

She woke up with a start some forty minutes later. It was nearly 6:30. Mrs. Brown had to make her calls. Bonnie would still be at her salon, but closing up soon.

What was Mrs. Brown frightened of? Did she really think that Bonnie would fire her? She did. Do you know how hard it is for women of a certain age, or a man for that matter, to get a job? Mrs. Brown couldn't afford to not work.

Mrs. Brown picked up the receiver of the white Princess phone in the guest room, held her breath, and dialed. Bonnie answered after three rings. With all the courage that she could muster, Mrs. Brown explained that her business in New York City was delayed. With great apologies, she said she would not be able to come to work tomorrow but would return the following day.

There was nervous-making silence at the other end of the phone.

"Well, please hurry back, Mrs. Brown. You've no idea what's happened here today," Bonnie said. "And I need you."

Mrs. Brown didn't know what to say. It was the first time Bonnie had ever said she was needed.

"I fired them all. The whole stinking, rotten bunch."

"You did what?" Mrs. Brown asked.

Bonnie had just discovered what Mrs. Brown had strongly suspected for some time. That Georgie and Francie and the other beauticians were stealing from the till.

They were taking tens and twenties here and there when Bonnie wasn't looking. When they knew Bonnie wouldn't be in the salon, they were doing clients' hair "off the books," not registering the appointments in the computer and then pocketing the money the customers paid them instead of putting it in the cash register.

Mrs. Brown had never said anything. How could she? It would be her word against theirs, and she thought Bonnie would never believe her, and probably fire her for telling the truth.

"I should have said something, but I didn't have any real evidence," Mrs. Brown said, and apologized.

Bonnie said there was no need to apologize. She understood the dilemma Mrs. Brown was in.

"They tried passing the blame on to you, Mrs. Brown," Bonnie said. "I am sorry to have to tell you this, but that's what they tried to do. But I knew better. It got plenty ugly here today with those fucking bitches. I had evidence. Mrs. Malvern" — she was one of Francie's regulars — "showed me seven — *seven!* — canceled checks she'd written for having her hair done seven different times without an appointment, without paying the salon directly."

Bonnie paused. "But enough about me. I was going to ask you first thing in the morning when you got here, so let me ask you now. How would you feel about getting your beautician's license? You're not too old, not really. I'll pay. I've seen that you have a great instinct for doing hair, and with just a bit of formal training, you will be my number one hairdresser. Hell, right now you'll be my only hairdresser.

"Please? I know I've been ratty to you when I should have been kind." Bonnie cleared her throat. "I'll turn over a new leaf, I promise. I even won't swear so fucking much in the salon." She added, "I mean, as much."

Mrs. Brown appreciated the effort.

"And your salary will be more, not to mention you keep all your tips," Bonnie said. She mentioned a number that was more than Mrs. Brown would ever have expected.

When Mrs. Brown hung up the telephone, she was stunned. What a day this had been! Wait until Mrs. Fox heard the news. She wouldn't write to her, she'd telephone her as soon as she got home tomorrow. In the meanwhile, she'd call Alice and explain that she wasn't coming back tonight.

CHAPTER 32

The 1970 Mercedes-Benz convertible was ruby red. It shone like a Christmas ornament, waxed and polished this afternoon in time for his date tonight.

Anthony got to East Seventy-fourth Street twenty minutes early. He tipped the doorman twenty dollars so he could stay parked in front of the awning of Rachel's building.

If he was going to impress Rachel, he believed it absolutely essential to act as cool as possible, but he was so nervous around her! Whether they were hipster kids or Social Register dowagers, the people in Rachel's society were the cool and aloof type. Sophisticated people suspicious of enthusiasm and trusting only that, and those, vetted and verified by some indecipherable code.

Here were Rachel and Mrs. Brown now under the awning.

"Your coach awaits, ladies," Anthony said.

His eyes were sapphire blue, his eyebrows brown as sable, his lips full, his smile, earnest and kind, demanding nothing in return. Must be the navy blazer he is wearing that's bringing up the blue of his eyes, Rachel thought, trying to think of something, anything, critical to mitigate her attraction to him. And there was the slightest hint of cologne, something wonderful. What was it? It was the smell of cedar after a summer rain.

It was unsettling to feel love's gravitational pull, and so soon.

"Rachel, the trouble with you, dear," her mother had told her when she was a bit too enamored of her high school French tutor, "is that you're the sort of girl who falls in love the way puppies slip in the mud. Which is constantly. Slip, and love will make you crazy, dear. Steady yourself. Develop some spine. Get a grip, girl."

When it came to men, Rachel got her grip. But she had taken her mother's caution too much to heart. She became very hard to get, and very few had gotten her. But how lonely she felt nowadays, something that her pride made hard to accept. In her mistaken estimation, only weak people admitted they were lonely.

"How could I be lonely," Rachel once

asked her boss when he inquired about her plans one weekend. "With all the great books I've still to read?"

Mrs. Brown insisted she sit in the backseat despite protests from both Anthony and Rachel. Especially Rachel, who believed her guest would see the city much better sitting up front next to Anthony.

"Never mind," said Mrs. Brown, getting into the backseat of the convertible. In her capacity as the evening's cupid, she knew what she was doing. Rachel sat in the front seat. Did Mrs. Brown just see Rachel blush? She certainly hoped so.

There were beige blankets folded perfectly on both seats.

"In case you get cold while we're driving," Anthony explained.

Mrs. Brown remembered seeing photographs of the Queen in her carriage, as well as in her limousine. Even in the warmer months, the monarch kept a blanket on her lap and over her knees. She must be susceptible to the cold, Mrs. Brown assumed. We all feel it more easily when we are older. (Fact is, the blanket is so that paparazzi do not capture any unladylike portion of royal leg or thigh.)

Horns, buses, taxis, adrenaline, bright lights, and a violet-blue September sky, it was a glorious night for a drive in the city. Mrs. Brown caught a glimpse of herself in the rearview mirror. Hardly her own greatest admirer, she liked what she saw. Mrs. Brown thought she'd never looked better than she did tonight.

Rachel turned around to Mrs. Brown and mouthed the words "our hair." She, too, had brought an Hermès scarf that had belonged to her grandmother. She tied it over her hair to hold it in place in the convertible. Mrs. Brown did the same.

Anthony described the route he had planned. He would drive east to the FDR Drive because it offered a terrific view of Manhattan from the vantage point of the East River, and then he'd drive southwest to catch the last of the sunset from the Financial District — did Mrs. Brown want to see where the World Trade Center had stood? She did — and then they would drive up to Times Square, and then up Eighth Avenue through Columbus Circle, and up Central Park West and Frederick Douglass Boulevard to the Great Blue Heron on 125th Street, where they had an 8:30 reservation.

After dinner, they'd drive down Fifth Avenue. Mrs. Brown had to see the Metropolitan Museum, "lit up at night, it looks like a huge white lion asleep," Anthony said, and then home by midnight if that wasn't too late?

"When we were kids, my father would take us for walks along the East River. We'd look for the seagulls," Anthony said, steering toward the East River now. "My father told us that New York City seagulls aren't just flying when they fly, they're also dancing. Man, did he love New York. When we got a little older, we realized most of the seagulls he was talking about were pigeons. We never asked him if he knew the difference. We didn't want to hurt his feelings."

The convertible raced along the FDR. There was a crescent moon over Manhattan. You could smell the briny river air mixing with Rachel's gardenia perfume. Riding in the convertible, Mrs. Brown felt exhilarated, light as the wind, younger and more unburdened than she had in many years.

Over the roaring chorus of wind and traffic, Anthony told stories about growing up here, about his family, his youth, and some of his best memories.

"It's so weird, but like your father, who said the seagulls were dancing, and the pigeons, our father told us something very similar," Rachel said. "We'd go to the beach on Long Island. He'd tell us that the sand was always dancing and that we should watch its dance, and if we were lucky enough to be asked by the sand to dance with it, we must."

Rachel pictured her father's smiling face but sad blue eyes. " 'It asked me, it asked me,' we'd cry out, absolutely delighted. We'd do these mad gyrations dancing with the sand until we were exhausted."

Rachel fell quiet, embarrassed to remember something so personal aloud.

Anthony imagined what Rachel must have looked like as a little girl. He wanted to reach across the white leather bucket seats and take her hand in his. Maybe later, he hoped. Maybe later.

For now, he told himself, keep both hands on the steering wheel and just drive, man, just drive.

CHAPTER 33

The day finally came for Mrs. Brown to take possession of her dress. Or at least she hoped it had finally come.

"You want to teach yourself to see good things coming, Emilia," her mother used to say. "Because God is always on the road ahead, sewing a tapestry of life for us."

Well, if the road last night wasn't godly, it certainly was divine. What a wonderful evening it had been on the town with Rachel and Anthony, and even though it had been decades since she had slept in a bed other than her own, to her surprise she had fallen right asleep when she got back to Rachel's just after 11:00 P.M.

Floating this morning in what had to be the most comfortable bed in the world, in Rachel's guest room, Mrs. Brown barely recognized her life! One day she was a woman who walks everywhere she goes in her Rhode Island town; last night she was zooming around Manhattan in a red Mercedes convertible.

They'd driven through Chinatown and Little Italy, Tribeca and SoHo, the West Village and Chelsea to West Forty-second Street. She'd never forget the density of people in New York, especially Times Square. The tall office buildings lit up like giants.

Over and up Eighth Avenue, then a loop around Columbus Circle, with its sparkling fountains — the horses and carriages were from a fairy tale — and up Central Park West, with its glorious apartment buildings and majestic Museum of Natural History. Then to dinner at the Great Blue Heron on 125th, where if everyone wasn't a movie star or a princess, they sure looked like one.

And the food: she ate crab cakes, oysters with ginger, country ham, chickpea dumplings, Creole red grits, and a spiced chocolate cake with rhubarb and brandied cherry vanilla sauce. Mrs. Brown, generally a teetotaler, even had a glass, a glass and a half to be exact, of a French rosé wine.

It was just as they were raising their glasses to toast each other that Delphine Staunton, all in black-layered summer cashmeres and bold scarlet lipstick, lurched over to their table.

This, Rachel knew, could be trouble. But before Delphine could get anything even approaching a nasty or snobbish word out, Rachel spoke first.

"Delphine, cheers, to your health," she said.

"To me?" Delphine asked. "Why?"

"We saw you coming," Rachel said.

Good manners make the best offense. Rachel had to act fast to stop Delphine from saying something hurtful to Mrs. Brown. Why is it some people's natures to always be disagreeable, unless they want something from you? So Rachel toasted Delphine's good health. What could Delphine do but thank her and respond with the best French bonhomie she was capable of?

As Delphine babbled a few words of thanks, Rachel courteously interrupted her.

"Isn't that Terry Killen the Third, the billionaire's son, just coming into the restaurant? You know his father just died, and I understand he's trying to figure out which auction house should deal with the estate. Delphine," Rachel said, "get right over there and say hello!"

Poof. Delphine was gone. And all Mrs. Brown thought of it was how nice it was to see someone she recognized in New York.

Now there was a knock on the guest room

286

door. Rachel entered carrying a breakfast tray.

"Breakfast in bed for all my honored guests from Ashville," she said, carefully setting the legs of the tray over Mrs. Brown's lap.

A white linen napkin, a white rose in a crystal vase, a blue and white porcelain pot of coffee, a small bowl of sugar, a tiny pitcher of milk, fresh fruit salad, and a warm morning glory muffin greeted Mrs. Brown.

"How many guests have you had from Ashville?"

"Only you, Mrs. Brown, and I hope you will come back," Rachel said.

What could bring Mrs. Brown back to New York? Rachel and Anthony's wedding would.

"He's nice," Mrs. Brown said.

"Who?" Rachel asked.

"Who? Your Anthony, that's who."

"My Anthony? I don't think so, not mine," Rachel said, dismissing the idea of anything serious between herself and Anthony Bruno.

But Mrs. Brown wasn't having it.

"Where's your coffee, dearie?" she asked Rachel. "Sit with me while I enjoy this delicious breakfast."

Rachel left the room and returned with a mug of black coffee and both her Black-

Berry and her iPhone. She sat in the cabbage-rose-chintz-covered Queen Anne chair across from Mrs. Brown's bed, and without makeup, her hair down and not yet brushed, barefoot and wearing a white tank top and faded blue jeans, she looked more like a fresh-faced college freshman than a big-city fashion executive.

"Last night you and Anthony got along quite nicely," Mrs. Brown said, and sipped her coffee. "He's a good man, Rachel, and they're hard to find. He's handsome, he loves and respects his family, and I imagine he makes a good living the way he described those fancy floors he puts in all these palatial apartments. What's so wrong with that?"

Rachel looked sad. "It's complicated. Really it is."

Before Mrs. Brown could inquire further, Rachel was saved from explaining exactly what was so complicated by the bell, or ping to be more exact, of her BlackBerry.

She read the message and smiled.

"They're here. *Brava! Bravi!* The two dresses have arrived at Kennedy Airport," she said. "They will be at the boutique by ten. It is a little after eight thirty now, and I am going to get dressed and work from my laptop here at home. Why don't you just take it easy? At ten or a little after we can walk down to the boutique. It's a lovely morning for a walk. You can try on the dresses and make your selection depending on which size fits you best."

When Rachel left, Mrs. Brown lay back in bed.

She closed her eyes and imagined what it would feel like when she finally saw the dress. Yet as wonderful as she expected the satisfaction of it to be, there was something else, a bittersweet feeling, the kind many feel after a personal victory of some sort. The dream is complete. What's next?

In the twenty-fours since she got to New York City, her fear of this place — once so foreign and overwhelming to her — had disappeared almost entirely. Thanks to Rachel's generosity, and also the other people who had helped her yesterday, she'd discovered that the city wasn't a forbidding kingdom, a roaring hungry lion waiting to eat her alive. It was a series of villages connected by a common thread of decency.

Just as in Ashville, here were mostly good people trying to live with some measure of dignity and grace. Not always succeeding, but always trying.

When she finally had her dress today, September 11, it would be time to leave, and she would miss this happy, muddled, difficult, glorious place.

Last night, when they had stopped to pay respects at the World Trade Center, in the everlasting sorrow of the place she also saw a state of grace. Gazing into the two thirty-foot waterfalls that seemed to drop into darkness in the footprints where the Twin Towers once stood, Mrs. Brown had felt — how should she describe it? — this presence in absence.

Instead of feeling separate, she felt she belonged. In loss, interlaced with others. No longer just someone tacked on to the tapestry called Life.

CHAPTER 34

By 10:30 that morning, Mrs. Brown was center stage at Oscar de la Renta. She was their phoenix rising.

The dressing room glittered with wall-around mirrors. Rachel sat in a chair busily tapping away on her telephones. It was Fashion Week, as you know, and she was "multitasking" she told Mrs. Brown as they awaited the arrival of Rachel's young assistant Daniel, who was bringing the dresses from the airport, one size eight and one size ten.

Ah, Daniel. If he were an oil portrait in a gilded frame the title would be *The Afternoon of a Faun*. A mop of dark-brown hair, wading pools of gray eyes with feathery lashes; wearing a white shirt and moss-green slim-fitting linen trousers cuffed above his ankles, no socks, and wing-tipped beige suede English brogues . . . Daniel entered. Not since Cleopatra was carried to Julius

291

Caesar in a rug had there been such devotion to presentation. Daniel held the two garment bags as if the dresses were made of the finest glass. The sort that anything less than a positive thought might shatter.

Rachel knew it was highly unlikely that either dress would fit Mrs. Brown without alteration. Despite so much to do in the workroom during Fashion Week, thanks to Rachel one of Oscar's best seamstresses would work exclusively on Mrs. Brown's dress so she could make her train back to Ashville. The seamstress stood at attention, waiting.

In the interim while the tailoring took place, Rachel had arranged a little surprise. As a present, Mrs. Brown would be getting her hair done today, plus manicure and pedicure, at the renowned Kenneth salon. Although it's closed now, at the time it was still enshrined at the Waldorf Astoria hotel.

The bags were unzipped, and out came two sizes of *the* dress, and two sizes of the notch-collared jacket that went with it. As if the sovereign in royal robes had just entered the room, the feeling of awe that she had experienced when she first saw this style in Mrs. Groton's closet returned. Mrs. Brown steadied herself.

Rachel nodded in Daniel's direction,

indicating it was time for Mrs. Brown to try on the dresses without male eyes on her.

"I'll be right outside if you need anything," he said.

Rachel suggested trying the size eight first. Mrs. Brown disrobed, carefully placing her gray trousers and brown twin-set on a lemon-yellow velvet chair. Who but Rachel right now had seen her so nearly naked in years? No one.

It was a ceremony practiced over the ages: the fitting. In high fashion, it's where the magic happens — well, if you are in the right hands. Mrs. Brown most certainly was.

Rachel held the black, light-wool-crepe sheath for Mrs. Brown. Mrs. Brown, right foot first, stepped into the dress. Rachel zipped the back zipper for her, but with difficulty.

Mrs. Brown looked in the three-way mirror, and her heart sank. The dress didn't fit. Mrs. Brown felt her disappointment deeply. To her, this was more than a dress. It was a calling.

Rachel whispered something to the seamstress that Mrs. Brown couldn't hear. "Let's try the size ten," she said.

The size ten was the charm. How wonderful the silk lining felt, but when the dress was zipped, it was too big.

What to do?

"Take it in, let it out, to be or not to be, I say go with the size ten," the seamstress finally said. She spoke with an accent Mrs. Brown couldn't place.

"You think that is better than working with the eight?" Rachel asked, her mobile phone beeping nonstop as it had all morning. "I thought the eight fit perfectly across the bosom. And we've got to try on the jackets, too."

The seamstress gave her a look. Translated, it said: get out of my kitchen.

Rachel laughed. "You're the boss, Irina."

Mrs. Brown, with her knowledge of sewing, knew that Irina had a lot of work to do. She worried how much it would cost. Even in Ashville the tailor at the dry cleaner's would probably charge at least one hundred dollars. How much, then, on Madison Avenue? Not to mention the time it would take.

Irina read Mrs. Brown's mind. "Four hours, including the jacket."

"Excellent," Rachel said.

Mrs. Brown didn't understand.

"It's eleven now? I can have this for you by three o'clock. You try on one more time and I make last fixes and then you go to train station in time, okay?" the seamstress asked.

"Yes, okay." Mrs. Brown was delighted. "But the cost . . ."

"Alterations are included, Mrs. Brown," Rachel said. She stepped out of the dressing room to take a call.

"We get to work," the seamstress said, her pins ready. "My name is Mrs. Novikov, Irina Novikov."

"How do you do, Mrs. Novikov, I am . . ."

Mrs. Novikov, pins in her mouth, interrupted: "I know who you are. You are famous in our office, even more than the fancy actresses we fit in the clothes."

She gestured with her jaw for Mrs. Brown to pivot. Mrs. Novikov continued pinching and pinning the dress.

"I am famous in your office? How's that?"

The seamstress looked Mrs. Brown in the eyes and gently nodded. "We heard about a woman maybe a lot like us, not from here, worked hard, saved her money so she could buy a lady's dress, and she traveled here her first time all alone to get it. And how Miss Ames, tough cookie, the ice princess, she melted. She helped you! She wouldn't always. Everyone is talking. Know why?"

"Why?"

"Everyone say Rachel Ames found her

heart yesterday thanks to you."

She continued pinning. Mrs. Brown was astonished by her expertise. "Women like us," Irina Novikov said, her voice sounding melancholy, "women like us, we are ladies, too, but no one sees us that way. We are invisible. But what do they see, what do they want? Baby dolls. Painted, silly, aging dolls. Women like us," she said, "we're treated like dead trees."

Mrs. Brown understood.

"But, ah, my friend, no one sees our roots, still growing, deeper and deeper." Mrs. Novikov adjusted the pins in her mouth and kept working, and talking.

"I have two sons fighting in the wars. Born here in America so they can go to war. I should dye my hair like a lemon, dress up like a Barbie doll, or spend all my money shopping, and save nothing? No. I am grown woman." She paused. "I'm the mother of two boys who are United States of America soldiers. The strongest limb on the tree bends so it won't break. I bend. I worry all day. I worry every night, but" — she pointed at her gray eyes with heavy lids and deep lines — "does anyone see my tears? Never, never here . . ."

Mrs. Brown put her right hand on Mrs. Novikov's shoulder for balance.

"It's going to be okay, dear," Mrs. No-vikov promised. "Put on the jacket now."

The jacket completed the regal picture. Its lining felt so soft, made of the finest silk imaginable. The shoulders of the size ten fit perfectly, but Mrs. Norikov said she wanted to take in the waist a bit and shorten the sleeves.

"It's not a problem. You have your dress at three today, and at three today you leave here a queen! Better than the movie stars! They have all the 'hoochie-coochie,' but you will have respect."

CHAPTER 35

At first Mrs. Brown questioned Rachel's invitation to have her hair done, a manicure and a pedicure, at the Kenneth salon. How much would it cost? At least four times what they charged at Bonnie's, and that wouldn't be cheap.

She needn't worry about the money. Rachel said the salon owed her a favor, and she'd appreciate the company as she was scheduled to have her hair done that day anyway.

"But everything," Mrs. Brown said, and hesitated. "A new dress, getting our hair done, you don't think, given what day it is, that it isn't in . . ."

"In bad taste?" Rachel said. "Because it's September eleventh?"

Mrs. Brown nodded. "Yes, that's what I'm thinking."

Rachel smiled. "What would Mrs. Groton do?"

Mrs. Brown liked the question but wasn't sure of the answer.

"She'd get her hair done, paint her face, put on her best dress, and show the bastards you can't keep a good woman down. And that's just what we're going to do today, Mrs. Brown. Okay?"

"Okay," Mrs. Brown said. "Okay!"

Rachel had a car and driver waiting to take them to the salon. As they walked to the car, Rachel remembered a favorite story Mrs. Groton had told her.

At the start of World War II, an editor for a newspaper called *PM,* no longer in print, wrote an editorial calling "for everything relating to fashion to be put on ice in penance until the war was won," Rachel said.

He singled out *Vogue* magazine. Why? Perhaps his wife was reading it when he woke up on the wrong side of the bed.

"What American people have to realize is that *Vogue* magazine, which only a few years ago was very real, is now only a temporary illusion," the editor wrote.

"He wanted the magazine to stop publishing out of respect for the troops and the struggles of their families living on rations at home," Rachel explained.

But the editor in chief of the fashion magazine, Edna Woolman Chase, didn't see things that way, not at all.

In defense of gracious living, one of American democracy's greatest freedoms, Mrs. Chase fired off a letter to the gentleman, and said: "We shall not be unmindful of the changing times. If the new order is to be one of sackcloth and ashes, we think some women will wear theirs with a difference! *Vogue* will cut the pattern for them, for we still believe that we shall survive."

Rachel opened the car door for Mrs. Brown. "That's real grit, isn't? Even if it's sackcloth, a strong woman wears hers with style."

Lexington Avenue was the quicker route, but Rachel wanted to enter the Waldorf at its main doorway, on Park Avenue, so Mrs. Brown could experience the full impact of the hotel's busy lobby.

On the way to the salon, Rachel explained that Kenneth Battelle had created hairstyles for Brooke Astor, Babe Paley, Katharine Graham, Gloria Vanderbilt, Jacqueline Kennedy, and Marilyn Monroe, but most famously, Mrs. Brown thought, he did Millicent Groton's hair.

Kenneth had visited Ashville on a number of occasions over the years. There had been an article about him, in *Vanity Fair* if Mrs. Brown remembered correctly, several years ago. All the women at Bonnie's had read it with great interest.

Rachel talked away but rarely looked up from her phones. "I really apologize for being so lost in my work today, but with Oscar's show coming up, there's so much to do, Mrs. Brown."

It was a bit of a lie. Crazy-busy Fashion Weeks were nothing new, and Rachel was supremely well organized. But she was coordinating one last surprise for Mrs. Brown. That is, if television's Charlie Rose didn't mind waiting fifteen minutes to tape his studio interview with Oscar this afternoon.

The Kenneth salon was even more splendid than Mrs. Brown could have imagined. And it was so quiet! Is that what real luxury is? Quietude? It isn't a loud three-ring circus somewhere? Compared to Bonnie's hysterics, cursing, and lousy TV at top volume, this was a Zen monastery in the Swiss Alps.

Handsome, hirsute, with thick beard and ginger features, Andy was the head hair man at the salon. He wore alligator clogs with silver pilgrim buckles and had eagles, balloons, and chains tattooed on his forearms. He closely examined Mrs. Brown's hair and proposed a light color rinse and feathered trim at the crown to add volume.

"But other than that I like your cut now," he said.

Her expression questioned his sincerity.

"I really do. Who does your hair, Mrs. Brown?" Andy asked.

She hesitated before answering, but why should she be embarrassed? Wasn't that one of the main messages she'd gotten since she arrived in New York City? Be yourself.

"I cut my own hair," Mrs. Brown said.

"I'm impressed!" Andy said.

She was pleased that he was impressed, especially considering her new hairdressing job at Bonnie's.

But you know what impressed Mrs. Brown most about Kenneth's? Coffee cups and teacups were covered with silver foil so any loose hair, scent, or hair spray didn't come anywhere near your beverage of choice. (Which in the case of the grande dame sitting next to Mrs. Brown today was a five-ounce glass of vodka on ice with a splash of fresh grapefruit juice that, at least in the mind of the grande dame, qualified the beverage as a health food drink.)

This kind of cleanliness and good order, along with the luxurious quiet, was the height of chic in Mrs. Brown's opinion.

With her hair done, nails manicured, and toes pedicured in clear matte polish, the only color she liked for herself, Mrs. Brown was declared "sublime." That was Rachel's word.

When they returned to the store on Sixty-sixth Street, Mrs. Brown was ushered to the changing room so quickly she didn't notice the small group of people clustered around a white-linen-covered table.

Mrs. Novikov was exhausted from working so hard and so fast, tailoring the dress and jacket in record time. She was also extremely pleased. As she helped Mrs. Brown into her new dress, with each millimeter of zip Mrs. Novikov's sense of pride grew.

"It's a miracle you could do this. But how did you do this?" Mrs. Brown asked. The tailoring was incredible.

"I've a few secrets?" Mrs. Novikov said, and laughed.

"It's like being held up by angels," Mrs. Brown said, rejoicing in the support of such a finely constructed dress. The matching jacket was just as edifying.

Rachel entered the dressing room carrying a pair of black croc leather pumps and a black cashmere cardigan sweater.

"You look wonderful, Mrs. Brown! How does the dress feel?" Rachel asked.

"I can't do it justice," Mrs. Brown answered. "I can't explain it. It feels as I hoped it would but even better."

Rachel asked Mrs. Brown to turn so she could inspect all aspects of the dress. "You did an exceptional job, Mrs. Novikov. Truly amazing."

"Yes, I did," Mrs. Novikov said.

"Oh," Rachel said, "these shoes. Try them on. They will go well with the dress. And also try this cardigan. Sometimes you won't want to wear the matching jacket. It's a good look, too, more modern than the jacket . . ."

The expression on Mrs. Novikov's face left no doubt that she disapproved of what Rachel was saying.

"With all due respect to the jacket and the dress combination. Oh, Mrs. Novikov, I mean no insult," Rachel said, and continued with her style counsel. "And if you want to make the dress even less formal, Mrs. Brown, you can try a color cardigan sweater instead of black. White is nice, red also."

Mrs. Brown stepped into the shoes and rose three inches in height and miles in confidence — funny thing how that always happens in a good pair of heels. Rachel held the cashmere cardigan open, and Mrs. Brown put it on, the softest thing she'd ever known.

After she paid for the dress, if she was going to save as much of the money from the sale of the hutch as she could, then she couldn't afford the shoes, but maybe the sweater? "How much is the sweater and how much are the shoes?" Mrs. Brown asked.

"Mrs. Brown, both are presents from me to you."

Mrs. Brown was not comfortable with this. "You mustn't, Rachel. I can't accept. You've done so much for me already. If I'm to have either, I must pay, really, I must."

"Mrs. Brown, I respect and appreciate what you are saying, but really I insist," Rachel said.

There was a polite standoff. Silence.

"Oh, go on, dearie, take 'em," Mrs. Novikov said.

"Well, let me go pay now and see what the total is. I want to pay for the sweater at least," Mrs. Brown said, and exited the changing room followed by Rachel and Mrs. Novikov.

Mrs. Brown noticed that a tall, dapper gentleman was coming toward her. He was very sophisticated, very tan, and very good looking.

"My goodness," he said in a Latin accent. "You look fantastic! Yesterday, when I first heard about you from Rachel, I didn't understand, why does this lady want this black dress? Sure this style is one of our biggest perennial sellers, but if you've saved your money, and you've taken all the trouble to make your first trip to New York to buy something from us, why not one of our more feminine numbers?"

This was the patron himself, the designer Oscar de la Renta.

Rachel had arranged for him to delay his interview with Charlie Rose for fifteen minutes so he could stop by the boutique to meet Mrs. Brown. Oscar wanted to personally present Mrs. Brown with one of his favorite alligator handbags. It would go so nicely with her new dress and shoes.

The designer introduced himself. "I'm Oscar. It's so good to see you, Mrs. Brown."

With all the old-world elegance for which he was famous, the designer took Mrs. Brown's hand and kissed it. Rachel had also organized a "champagne reception" — the buffet table in the front of the store had buckets of champagne and little pastries on a tiered silver server. Oscar didn't let go, but sweetly held Mrs. Brown's hand in his until a bottle of champagne was uncorked with a thunderous pop and everyone applauded.

Glasses were filled. Oscar proposed a toast

to Mrs. Brown's health and safe trip home. He thanked her "for honoring us with your excellent choice in dresses."

He made a short speech. Oscar said that when fashion becomes too big a business, a designer might forget the reason he got into it in the first place: to make a lady's life happier, and to give her confidence.

"You've reminded us what our primary purpose is." Oscar took Mrs. Brown's hand and kissed it. "And we all thank you."

Mrs. Brown was stunned. "No," she said, almost pleading. "I thank you. I thank all of you so much."

It was Rachel's turn to say something to Mrs. Brown. "Since I saw you yesterday, I've felt I have a new pair of glasses. Knowing you, Mrs. Brown, even for such a short time, has meant so much to me."

"But you don't wear glasses," Mrs. Brown said.

"Okay, then, a new pair of contact lenses." Rachel laughed. She embraced Mrs. Brown.

Over Rachel's shoulder Mrs. Brown saw Anthony Bruno entering the store and, through the glass storefront, his red Mercedes convertible waiting. He was driving her to Penn Station.

It was time to say goodbye to these sweet people.

Anthony greeted Mrs. Brown. Rachel introduced him to Oscar de la Renta. But they'd already met, which astonished Rachel. Anthony's company had done the floors at the designer's country house, and both men, as they discovered, were avid fans of mariachi music. Someday, Anthony promised, he would sing for Rachel (at our wedding, he was thinking).

Mrs. Brown asked one of the salespeople for the bill for her purchases. When it was presented, there was a big mistake. It said the amount Mrs. Brown owed was half of what she expected to pay.

"What's this?" Mrs. Brown asked. "It must be some mistake."

The salesperson didn't know how best to respond, but here was Oscar de la Renta to help.

"We've an expression on Seventh Avenue. It's music to most women's ears. 'I can get it for you wholesale,' and, Mrs. Brown," Oscar said, "if I can't get it for you wholesale, then we're in a lot of trouble around here."

With that, he said his goodbyes.

The better it gets, the better it gets; Mrs. Brown couldn't believe her good fortune and everyone's kindness. While she changed back into her traveling clothes, her dress was packed in tissue inside an Oscar de la Renta dress box. It was wrapped with ribbons and tied with handles for her to carry.

Given that she had a considerable amount of money left over, she wanted to buy something for Mrs. Fox and for Alice. She noticed a gold bracelet with one charm on it, the designer's initials, ODLR. That seemed perfect. Something Mrs. Fox would never buy for herself, that glittered, and that felt "very New York," in the words of Rachel's assistant, Daniel, who wholeheartedly approved the purchase.

It was harder to choose something for Alice. Mrs. Brown decided on a navy blue enamel frame about five inches square. It was a handsome frame, and she could imagine the note she could write when she presented it. Something along the lines of "For your favorite photograph of Milo." Clearly, Alice was falling in love with him, and Mrs. Brown wanted to be encouraging.

"I'm going to come visit you! Okay?" Daniel exclaimed.

Why not? "Please do," Mrs. Brown said. "Do you like hair salons? I think Bonnie would like you."

"Do I like hair salons?" Daniel responded. "Y-E-S! Clothes stores, spas, hair salons, they're my churches, Mrs. Brown."

Mrs. Novikov was heading back to the dressing room to gather her sewing things. Mrs. Brown stopped her. She took her hand and pressed a hundred-dollar bill inside. Maybe not for the famously rich one percent, but for everyone else a hundred dollars was still a lot of money. And Mrs. Brown, having the sewing skills that she did, knew how masterful Mrs. Novikov's talent was.

"What's this?" Mrs. Novikov asked.

"I want to thank you is all," Mrs. Brown said.

Mrs. Novikov unfolded the bill. "A tip?"

Mrs. Brown worried that she had offended her, the last thing she intended. But she knew how nice it was, and rare, to receive a truly generous gratuity for a job well done.

"I hope I didn't offend you?" Mrs. Brown said.

"Offend me?" Mrs. Novikov smiled. "Not at all. You're a good woman, Emilia Brown. I wish there were more like you around."

Anthony brought Mrs. Brown's dress box to his car. Rachel said she would overnight the handbag, shoes, and cardigan because they would be too much for Mrs. Brown to manage on the train. Daniel had packed a picnic supper, chicken salad sandwiches with bacon and two small bottles of Evian water, for Mrs. Brown's trip to Ashville.

There were hugs and smiles and promises to be in touch. Even the salespeople who had been so suspicious when they first saw her enter their emporium yesterday were sad to see Mrs. Brown leave. After all, they were just doing their jobs and now regretted the rush to judgment.

Rachel's eyes filled with tears. She insisted Mrs. Brown promise to come back to New York City to visit. Rachel and Mrs. Brown hugged one more time. When Rachel said goodbye to Anthony, instead of giving him a kiss, she shook his hand.

Mrs. Brown wasn't pleased to observe this, but she was ready with a plan. She conveniently forgot to return the set of apartment keys Rachel had given her yesterday when she went to her office, in case Mrs. Brown wanted to go for a walk.

Just as Anthony drove up to the Seventh Avenue entrance to Pennsylvania Station, Mrs. Brown decided it was the perfect time to remember the keys.

"Oh, good Lord," she said. "I've kept Rachel's apartment keys by mistake." She pressed the keys into Anthony's hand. "Will you please return them for me as soon as possible? Rachel will be so worried that they are lost."

Anthony nodded that he would.

"She won't feel safe until you put them in her hand yourself."

"Yes, of course, Mrs. Brown. I will."

"And, Anthony," Mrs. Brown said, stepping onto the sidewalk, "when you telephone, and I do mean telephone, not text, Rachel about the keys, don't let her tell you to leave them with her doorman. You understand? You return them over a nice dinner in a quiet, romantic restaurant, not one of those places that are so noisy you can't hear your heart."

Anthony smiled. He understood her plan. "You bet I will!" He came around the car and hugged her so affectionately that he lifted her off the sidewalk. "Thanks, Mrs. Brown. Thank you!"

CHAPTER 36

Alice sat at Mrs. Brown's kitchen table, Santo, the cat, asleep in her lap, and waited for her friend's return home.

Alice had barely breathed a decent breath since receiving Mrs. Brown's telephone call yesterday afternoon saying she wasn't coming back to Ashville last night. Even if she might have been able to relax, her grandmother's anxiety was overwhelming. They'd conferred on the telephone right after Alice got Mrs. Brown's call.

Mrs. Brown had explained everything. In theory it all made sense. That she had to stay in New York until the jacket and dress in her size options arrived from another boutique, that she had been offered a fine place to stay with the young woman who was once Mrs. Groton's assistant. They had met during the inventory of the great lady's things. Hadn't she told Alice all about Rachel Ames? How was this for a small world?

She now works for Oscar de la Renta. She had come to Mrs. Brown's rescue.

Yes, Alice remembered hearing about Rachel, but still. She worried. Mrs. Brown at night in a stranger's apartment in New York City? She might have protested Mrs. Brown's decision except for one thing. She didn't often admit it, but she'd become a daily devotee of the horoscope in the *Ashville Bulletin*. Her grandmother hadn't stopped delivery of the paper before she went to Vancouver, and Alice checked the horoscope every day before going to work.

Yesterday it had advised her to "keep your nose out of what other people do. Leave them to sort out their own dilemmas while you get on with your life."

With this in mind, she kept her lips buttoned and simply thanked Mrs. Brown for the alert and wished her a wonderful night in the city. Then she'd read this bit of ink-stained astrological advice to her grandmother to keep her calm. It hadn't worked. Mrs. Fox was sleepless in Vancouver last night, awake worrying.

Now, tonight, if all went according to today's plan — which she assumed it had because if it hadn't, surely Mrs. Brown would have telephoned — Mrs. Brown should have been here four minutes ago!

How ridiculous it had seemed to Alice when Mrs. Brown first declared her intention to save for the Oscar de la Renta dress. How many weeks — months actually — did it take her to finally realize that for Mrs. Brown this wasn't ridiculous, or frivolous, that she was experiencing something profound?

Alice wished she'd been less judgmental and more supportive from the start. She could have been more enthusiastic. But the one thing she was glad for was that she had never told, and never would tell, Mrs. Brown how Paul Gallico's *Mrs. 'Arris Goes to Paris,* the book that had so inspired her, ends.

It may offer an enlightened ending, but not a happy one, certainly not for the dress.

Soon after Mrs. 'Arris returns to London from Paris, a spoiled rich girl Mrs. 'Arris cleans for is in a state of despair about what to wear to an important event where she must make a good impression on a well-heeled suitor. The too kind and too generous Mrs. 'Arris lends her dress — which she herself has yet to wear. Hours of party-going later, the dress is irreparably ruined, and the rich girl just leaves it in a pile for Mrs. 'Arris to find when she comes in to clean.

Was this a bad omen for Mrs. Brown's dress? Doomed by the folly of its acquisition? That's what worried Alice.

But Alice never said a word.

CHAPTER 37

It was after three in the morning when Mrs. Brown finished telling Alice the story of her day and night in the city.

Alice had heard footsteps on the sidewalk just after midnight. The bountiful Oscar de la Renta dress box was so big it had to enter the house first. Mrs. Brown presented the blue enamel picture frame, and it was much appreciated for the reasons Mrs. Brown had hoped. The bracelet for Mrs. Fox, wrapped by Daniel, was described and then put on a high shelf in the closed kitchen cupboard where Santo couldn't get to it.

Next, the pièce de résistance: the dress box was opened and the dress and jacket examined on its hanger as if they were treasures just discovered on an archaeological dig at one of the great temples in Greece.

Mrs. Brown told Alice all about the lucky occurrences and blessed coincidences that had made the past forty-eight hours not only possible, but also irresistible.

She described everything about the city, from the birds in its trees to the gum on its sidewalks, and told of the wonderful circus of people everywhere, the shock of ending up at a fashion show, her tears when she was told her dress wasn't in stock, the miracle of seeing Rachel Ames again, her kindness and hospitality, and then all about Mrs. Brown's matchmaking efforts when Anthony Bruno entered the picture.

"Really, a young Marlon Brando?" Alice said, repeating Mrs. Brown's description of Anthony.

The dress and jacket hung on their plush hanger over the kitchen door leading to the living room.

"Well, will you try the dress on so I can see it on you, Mrs. Brown?" Alice asked.

She shook her head. "Another night," Mrs. Brown said.

Alice sighed. "Please, Mrs. Brown!"

Mrs. Brown wasn't moving.

"It's not a dress to model," Mrs. Brown said. "I just want to look at it for a while."

Finally, too tired to talk more, they agreed to resume tomorrow. They said their good nights.

Mrs. Brown moved the dress to her bedroom door. When she woke up in the morning, just a few hours from now, it would be the first thing she saw.

Her sleep was not simple, or easy. Her dreams were elaborate and colorful, all these tumbling, whirling images. At one point Anthony's red Mercedes convertible was a stagecoach doubling as a hovercraft making crazy-eight shapes over Manhattan, like a bucking moon in need of a lasso, or a cowboy, maybe both.

At 7:00 A.M. — an hour later than was usual on a workday — she woke up. Here was Santo's nose to her nose, and there across the room, hanging on the bedroom door, was the prized dress, proof that yesterday was real, not a dream.

Blurry eyed from just a few hours of sleep but eager and energized nonetheless, Mrs. Brown arrived at Bonnie's and assumed her new role as the second in command in the salon.

It was difficult at first — some of the customers were disinclined to trust the cleaning lady with their hair — but Mrs. Brown, in her quiet, steady, and uncomplaining way, eventually won them over.

"What would Mrs. Groton do?" she'd ask herself whenever she needed guidance and confidence.

When the rest of the things from New York

— the shoes, the new handbag, and the cashmere cardigan sweater — arrived, Mrs. Brown unpacked them and found them honored places in her closet. (After a month of keeping the dress displayed on its hanger on her bedroom door, she finally put it in her closet, out of sight but rarely out of mind.)

Rachel Ames telephoned Mrs. Brown several days after her return to Ashville, to make sure she was well and that everything had arrived okay. And also to mention that she had had dinner with Anthony Bruno already twice that week, and was seeing him for dinner that night. She thanked Mrs. Brown for coming up with the idea of giving her keys to Anthony to return, to make sure they connected again.

"What do you mean? I didn't plan that," Mrs. Brown said.

"Okay, Mrs. Brown, whatever you say."

A few weeks later, when Rachel called again, things had advanced from dinners to entire weekends with Anthony. In fact, the day after Thanksgiving they thought it would be fun to come for the weekend, staying at the Ashville Inn, which reopened that fall, and wondered if Mrs. Brown would be free to join them, as their guest, for dinner on the Saturday night.

"With your neighbor Alice, too," Rachel said. "We'd love to meet her, and her grandmother if she's back from Vancouver."

Mrs. Brown was delighted to accept, and Alice was thrilled. But no one, including Mrs. Fox, knew when she'd return to Ashville.

Whenever Mrs. Brown thought of New York or heard it mentioned somewhere, she felt joyful.

She looked forward to seeing her young New York City friends again. And when she heard on the evening news that Oscar de la Renta had died after a long illness — meaning that when he'd been so gracious and debonair with her he was not in good health but bravely soldiering on one day at a time, facing the loss of his life and the work that he so loved — she cried.

CHAPTER 38

On Mother's Day, Mrs. Brown finally wore her dress.

It was a cool but not cold Sunday afternoon. There were few buds and new leaves, but there was green lawn, sparrows, and forsythia.

Mrs. Brown awakened early, at 5:30 that morning. She made her tea and fed Santo and, taking her teacup back into her bedroom, sat at the edge of her bed and studied the framed photographs on her bedside table. Her parents, long gone, and Mr. Brown. "God rest their souls," Mrs. Brown whispered. She returned the pictures to the drawer.

For a long while she held one last photograph to her heart. "Happy Mother's Day," she said, and kissed it so gently. Then, instead of putting it away with the others, she left it on the table.

Santo finished his meal in the kitchen and

sat at her feet, his head cocked, looking up at Mrs. Brown.

"I'm going to wear the dress, Santo, I think today is the right day," she said.

Mrs. Brown bathed and fixed her hair. She applied her makeup, a very light foundation, a touch of powder, and a tiny bit of mascara. Her lipstick was a light pink matte, barely detectable. She dabbed on a very little bit of the same gardenia scent that Rachel Ames wore. Rachel had given her a small bottle of it to remember her by.

Mrs. Brown took the fine black dress from her closet and hung it on a peg on the back of the bedroom door. She removed her robe, put on her intimate wear, including a new pair of good sheer stockings, and then took the dress from its hanger and stepped into it, a portal to another world, which it was, a different countenance for Mrs. Brown.

As the dress became her, and as she became the dress, Mrs. Brown's posture straightened. She rose even taller when she stepped into the black pumps that Rachel had selected for her. She debated whether to wear the jacket or the cashmere cardigan sweater and decided on the jacket. She slipped her arms inside its sleeves, her bare arms soothed by the silk lining.

Mrs. Brown was ready. She stood for inspection in her full-length mirror.

She exhaled.

The pleasure she felt was not her vanity, although the tailored black sheath, the handsome jacket with the notched collar and one perfect button, and the high-heeled pumps that flattered her legs all made her look so elegant.

The feeling was composure, a quiet satisfaction, a sense of accomplishment, of purpose and dignity. This fed her heart in ways she could never, nor would ever try to explain, lest someone think she was bragging instead of expressing her deepest gratitude.

In the mirror, Mrs. Brown saw a picture that had been wanting for its ideal frame for a very long time.

She had her mother's Sunday gloves and a crisp, clean white handkerchief in her pocketbook. Taking one last deep breath, she exhaled, looking into the mirror. Mrs. Brown knelt down and passed her hand over Santo's furry head, and then she was out the door.

Alice, in her kitchen making the morning coffee, heard Mrs. Brown's footsteps. Milo was still dozing in her bed, and she woke him. From her living room window, they watched Mrs. Brown walk east toward the village.

"Look," they said at the same moment, "she's finally wearing the dress."

Seeing Mrs. Brown so regal and beautiful? Alice didn't attempt to stop the tears of gratitude that fell from her eyes, nor could she have even if she had tried.

Milo held Alice in his arms. From his memory of a favorite poem came this, which he whispered:

"We can be still,
So still we start to know
The depth of everything,
So still we hear the stars
Begin to sing. . . ."

Mrs. Brown did not go unnoticed as she passed through the village.

Despite the early hour, and the quiet of Mother's Day morning, a number of Ashville's townspeople found themselves at their windows, or in their front yards, at the moment when Mrs. Brown walked past.

Those who knew, bowed their heads.

It was twenty minutes to nine. Mrs. Brown walked east, the sun still finding its way into the day. Across Main Street, the village green and rose garden, and past the three oldest churches in Ashville — Episcopal, Methodist, and Presbyterian, where people were arriving for the early services — Mrs. Brown walked.

Past white clapboard and brown shingle houses built in the seventeen and early eighteen hundreds, and past the Catholic church, she was tall. She was purposeful.

At the edge of Ashville village, after walking across the town's landmark covered bridge, Mrs. Brown came to the cemetery.

She opened the rusty latch on the wrought-iron gate. She entered the graveyard. There was the sharp smell of pine needles and the melancholy scent of damp leaves. The ground was wavering, still wet from morning, but instinctively she knew how to negotiate in high heels, to not sink in, walking on the balls of her feet, gliding like a swan over quicksand.

When she saw the gravestone, she didn't cave. Like any good mother through the history of time, when her child comes home wounded from a fall, no matter how bloody, she faced the pain and remained fully present. Her heart opened.

The gravestone read:

ROBERT CHRISTOPHER BROWN

LCpl
United States Marine Corps
July 18 1978
January 25 2008
Purple Heart Operation
Iraqi Freedom
Beloved Son

It had started with three deadening raps on her front door, and their echo, knocking, evermore.

The bleak winter night when she got the news, delivered to her by two men in uniform, that Robert, or Robbie as she always called him, had been killed by an IED, an improvised explosive device, in the Anbar province in western Iraq. What could she do? She thanked the soldiers for stopping. She offered them a glass of water.

They declined.

She closed the door.

Mrs. Brown tidied up and then went straight to her bed convinced that she would wake up in the morning and discover, if she even remembered it, that it had all been a dream.

In the morning, it wasn't a dream.

Within seventy-two hours, the remains of

Robert Christopher Brown were returned to the United States.

Robbie could have been buried at Arlington National Cemetery, but Mrs. Brown knew she wouldn't be able to visit him there whenever she wanted. It was too far away. Instead, there was an honor guard detail for the burial in Ashville, the full military funeral honors, which are provided by law when the family requests them.

The day of the funeral, a convoy bearing Robbie's coffin traveled to Ashville from the airport in Providence. Rows of mourners had lined the village's Main Street, not unlike the line she stood in when Mrs. Groton had buried her son, David, so many years ago. Getting into the car the funeral parlor sent for her today, Mrs. Brown remembered the crackling sounds of slow wheels on dry leaves when David's hearse went by. She saw Mrs. Groton's gloved hand on the flag on his coffin.

Robbie wasn't the most popular boy at Ashville High School. He was that boy who couldn't wait until he was old enough to join the service and see the world, a world that had to be, he'd hoped, an easier, bigger place than here. But the people of Ashville, young and old, turned out to pay their respects to the fallen hero.

It was so bright and sunny that day, it was cruel. A bugler played taps. When the flag that covered Robbie's coffin was folded and presented to her, Mrs. Brown was numb. She was holding the flag like you would a baby in your arms, looking across the cemetery as the coffin was being lowered into its grave, and seeing tears streaming from Mrs. Fox's eyes. She wondered why. What could the matter be? And then she remembered.

Mrs. Brown kept the flag in her bedside table along with Robbie's photograph and the other photographs she displayed every night before she went to sleep.

One Sunday afternoon a few months after the funeral, she was in her kitchen when she heard someone knocking on her front door. She opened the door, and there stood a Marine who said he was Robbie's best friend in Iraq and had been nearby when he was killed.

The Marine was carrying a perforated vinyl case, and inside was a cat. It was Santo, that cat that Robbie had found and adopted in Iraq. Hadn't Robbie written to Mrs. Brown about Santo? Indeed, he had. Did Mrs. Brown want the cat? If she didn't, he'd keep him, although his mother, in New London, where he would be staying for a while, was allergic.

"But I just thought, you know . . . I am so sorry, Mrs. Brown," he said, tears in his eyes. He had been Robbie's best friend, he said again.

The moment the soldier opened the case, Santo jumped into Mrs. Brown's lap as if he'd always been here.

Sunday mornings, even in the deepest snow or heaviest rain, and from the first Sunday after the funeral, Mrs. Brown walked to Robbie's grave and prayed. When she was finished praying, she would tell Robbie about her week.

Yes, she still believed in God. As she always had, she believed that the purpose of a human's life was to prove that God exists, and how you did that was by practicing courtesy and kindness in all your affairs, always, no matter your circumstances, hurt, or pain, and through any crisis of faith.

That first year after Robbie was killed, it took all the strength and energy that she could muster, or fake, to get to the cemetery and then back home again. She was always so tired. What is the matter with me, she'd ask herself over and over. Mrs. Fox, who watched closely over her friend and neighbor, thought it was a miracle that Mrs. Brown managed to go to work, never missing a single day.

Then came the afternoon at Mrs. Groton's when Mrs. Brown saw the dress and jacket that took her breath away, and the idea was born in her. This is what she felt she needed: a dress as strong as armor.

She believed the dress would carry her with dignity and grace specifically on Sundays, when she visited Robbie's grave. *This is what I must wear.*

Sometimes she doubted her right to have such a dress. Who did she think she was? The First Lady? Mrs. Groton? The Queen of England? No. She was Robert Christopher Brown's mother.

Robbie would be comforted, not to mention so very proud, to see his mother here today looking this well.

She liked a Jewish tradition she had heard Bonnie talking about. When you go to a grave, place a stone on it so the departed one will know that you have visited. Before she had entered the graveyard, outside the gate, Mrs. Brown had found a nearly heart-shaped stone she rested now in just the right place.

She faced Robbie's headstone and looked at it deeply, as if it had eyes. She smoothed the folds of the new black dress. As if he were here now, resting on the sofa at home chatting away after his favorite Sunday breakfast (pancakes, three eggs sunny-side up, and bacon), Mrs. Brown told Robbie the full story of her day, and night, in New York. She laughed and gushed and did not edit a word.

Always on Sundays, memory's scissors cut sharp at her heart. Always on Sundays came the time to let the tears drop. And they did.

Except now the perfect black dress helped her to remember who she was. Who Robbie was, and the family they were. Like her rod and her staff, the dress gave her the courage to confront the shadows of death. She felt love, and she felt peace, both in shadow and in light, filling her heart.

"If I could have changed the world," Mrs. Brown said quietly, facing the memory of her son, "I would have stopped all time so you could stay."

The sun had done all it could do for her today. Mrs. Brown felt a chill. She wrapped her arms around herself and straightened her shoulders for the journey home.

And, yes, she looked divine.

ABOUT THE AUTHOR

William Norwich is a writer and editor and video and television reporter. As a journalist, he has written for *Vogue, Vanity Fair, The New York Times, The New York Observer,* and many other publications. He is currently the commissioning editor for fashion and interior design at Phaidon Press. He received an MFA in creative writing from Columbia University and is the author of the novel *Learning to Drive.* He lives in New York City.

The employees of Thorndike Press hope you have enjoyed this Large Print book. All our Thorndike, Wheeler, and Kennebec Large Print titles are designed for easy reading, and all our books are made to last. Other Thorndike Press Large Print books are available at your library, through selected bookstores, or directly from us.

For information about titles, please call:
  (800) 223-1244

or visit our Web site at:
  http://gale.cengage.com/thorndike

To share your comments, please write:
  Publisher
  Thorndike Press
  10 Water St., Suite 310
  Waterville, ME 04901